CASTAWAY TRANSFORMATIONS

James Owens

For Mom and Dad

CHAPTER ONE

Fishing

"Linot."

Linot woke and opened his eyes, his slight movement causing his hammock to sway. It was dark inside the hut, and from all around he could hear the sound of his family sleeping. No light of dawn intruded through the doorway, but Linot knew it was time to start the day. He paused just a moment, wondering whose voice had awakened him. There was no one near, no one else awake yet. Linot did not believe in spirits, so it must have been a dream. He slipped feet first out of his hammock. Standing there, he waited for the memory of the new day's business to come to him, and then frowned when it did. "Mundan," he muttered in disgust and shook his head.

The spring was a cold one, in Linot's opinion, and he wrapped his robe around his bare body. Some of the other villagers had already adopted the traditional nakedness of summer, but Linot was not ready for that. He strapped on his belt and checked to be sure his knife was still secure in it. Taking his sailor's pack Linot stepped around his sleeping siblings and left the hut, heading for the great house. The light of dawn had not yet touched the square bulk of the great house, with its sacred shrines and public bath, but Linot did not need to see it to find it. As the son and pupil of the chief's scribe, Linot did not spend his summers at sea, but rather stayed on his home island of Nemdahod, and so knew the paths by heart. He wound his usual way through the village to the large building. Once there he stopped at the well in front of the spirit face to fill his water gourd, grabbed some roasted tubers off the nearby altar of a lesser god, then headed inside to the fisherman's shrine. A lone, standing figure could be made out in the faint light of the single torch. As Linot approached the dim light allowed him to see it was Mundan, the old man he was to go fishing with that day. He looked up as Linot approached. Linot's nose wrinkled at a pungent odor. He thought at first it was Mundan's, and then he saw the bucket of bait in the older man's hands.

"We must go," Mundan said. "The wind spirits will not be pleased with us if they find us on the beach at dawn." With that Mundan walked toward the exit. Linot just nodded and followed the older man as he headed towards the shore where the villagers had beached the fishing canoes. Further out, in the center of the lagoon, a large black silhouette stood against the sky. Linot's eyes did not want to leave it. It was a foreign vessel, one of the few Linot had ever seen. A light on its deck allowed Linot's fascinated gaze to study the oddly-shaped ship for a moment. Its shape and bulk were unlike anything he had seen before, and Linot's pulse quickened as he strained to make out any details in the black silhouette. It was as if a giant door had opened to the underworld right in the center of the lagoon. Linot's eye spotted a man walking a watch on the deck, and he reminded himself that it was a boat, made of wood and rope and fabric -- like their own, just larger. He deliberately turned away, looking down the path toward the beach.

Few of the other villagers were up yet, and the two men reached the boats without further conversation. Linot hesitated, waiting to see which of the boats Mundan would go to, then followed the old man to where one of the smaller boats awaited. It was a narrow dugout, hollowed from a tree and polished with sap. It had a single outrigger, and only four seats. A single icon was carved on each side of the bow and stern, unlike the highly-decorated hulls of a war canoe or trading boat. Climbing inside,

Linot began to check the contents, silently reciting the litany each sailor was taught as a boy, tallying the oars and lines and gear. He was halfway through when he realized Mundan was still standing at the bow of the ship, staring at him. He stared back for a moment, puzzled, then realized that Mundan wanted to say the ritual prayer of casting off. Linot's father had taught him the prayer, but did not always use it himself, and Linot had little time for it. Mundan was staring intently, however, so Linot sighed and made the ritual opening gestures. He then had to wait as Mundan did the rest of the motions and chanted the words, not seeming to be in any hurry to finish. Linot was not sure, but it almost seemed like Mundan added an extra verse. Finally, it was done. "Push off," Mundan then said, seizing the bow of the boat and shoving. Linot dug into the sand with his oar and leaned back, easing the bow up. The boat slid across the sand, Mundan climbed in, and they were away.

Linot was not happy to have Mundan as a fishing partner. The old man was slow and weak and far too superstitious for Linot's taste. He would rather have been fishing with his father, who made no effort to placate any spirits before pushing off in the morning. Linot's father had left the morning before, however, to join a potlatch on Sanduha, a nearby island. He would be gone for many days, and the family needed fish. It took at least two to operate a fishing boat, and so Mundan agreed to take Linot out. The boat was small and fast, and the two had no problems moving it quickly through the lagoon. As they passed the looming shadow of the foreign ship, Mundan made a sign to ward off evil. Reflexively, Linot almost did as well, but then shook his hand instead and stared directly at the ship, noting the many lines and smelling the strange mineral odor of the hull. Then they were past it, and open water lay ahead. They paddled hard up the channel toward the reef, taking care to stay in the channel. On either side waves broke over dangerous shoals. The remnants of a wrecked canoe were entangled on one. Mundan again made a magical sign, but Linot decided to use his hands to paddle harder. Dawn found them in deep water. Linot chafed impatiently as Mundan chanted a prayer over the gear, and then he and the older man cast their baited lines.

The day remained gray and cold. Linot shivered occasionally as he worked, even with his robe to warm him. He wondered how Mundan, naked save for his belt and some fetishes, could handle the ocean chill. Mundan seemed to be more worried about the currents and the waves. Every so often he would stand up and scan the horizon. "Pirates," he said when he saw Linot scowling at him. Linot just shook his head at the crazy old man and kept casting. The action was good, but the catch was thin. Linot's hooks kept breaking, or getting stripped of their bait. Mundan was doing even worse. When the nibbles on the lines quieted in one spot, Mundan and Linot would paddle to another, usually near submerged reefs. Eventually Linot had enough fish for the day. Mundan had not gotten his baskets full yet, though, so Linot started fishing for him as well. Seeing this, Mundan actually stopped fishing and started counting the waves. This irritated Linot so much he almost stopped fishing, until he realized that he had no idea where the island was.

Linot stood up in the boat and scanned the horizon, but the waves and the clouds were all he could see. He realized that for all his journeys out to fish, he had never been this far out in a boat this low to the water. He looked at Mundan, who was also standing. "The waves are wrong," Mundan said. Linot looked on as the older man pointed at the patterns the waves were making. "The crossover should be less angled." Mundan lifted one foot and set it on the side of the canoe, looking out across the waves. Linot sat down and waited, trying to ignore the fear in his stomach. He stared up at the old man, noticing for the first time that many of the red and black tattoos that covered Mundan's brown, wrinkled skin from neck to knee were of sharks and storms and death. After a long pause Mundan spoke. "We are too near the shoals. We need to move away from them to see the true pattern of the waves. Start paddling."

Fear lent strength to Linot's arms, and the small canoe responded nicely to the efforts of the two men with the oars. The wooden hull cut through the water almost silently, and with every crested wave Linot felt sure they were drawing closer to home. Too soon, however, he heard the sound of waves breaking. Mundan again stood at the prow as the canoe came upon a small island of coral, one of dozens scattered in the waters around the big island. He pointed to where a tiny cove sheltered a sliver of sand.

"We will beach the boat," Mundan said, "and I will climb up and try to see the island." He studied the small rocky outcropping. "There will be fish trapped in the pools here. See what you can gather." Linot nodded, unhappy with the assignment but too worried to usurp the elder's authority. Linot wished his father were here, in the big canoe with all the other men, but at the same time assuring himself that for all his foolish superstition, Mundan still knew how to navigate, a skill Linot had yet to master. He waited for Mundan to aim the bow of the dugout at the cove, then laid into the paddle. Their efforts drove the boat up the shore, away from the waves, and both scrambled out and dragged the canoe up far from the reach of the water. Mundan fixed his gaze on Linot. "Watch out for island spirits." Mundan turned away to climb over the sharp rock. Linot nodded vigorously, then shook his head at the old man's weird and contagious superstitions. He pulled off his cape and tossed it in the dugout, took his pack, then began to circle the island and look for more food.

This task proved tricky as the landscape was nothing more than a heap of coral boulders, each one presenting a thousand shattered edges to cut and bruise the careless traveler. After a few minutes of painful trekking Linot found a large tidal pool, and he could see fish darting back and forth in it. He climbed down into it and set to work. As he fished, Linot occasionally climbed back up and looked around. The footing was slow and uncertain, and Linot slipped repeatedly onto the edges and blades of rock. Sometimes, when he looked, he saw Mundan standing atop various tall boulders, and sometimes he just saw the naked boulders. A glance across the horizon showed no signs of the main island. His cuts stung, and it was not long before his own blood mingled with the blood of his catch and ran down his belly and loins in thin rivulets. Had he still been wearing his robe it would have been in tatters. His thoughts kept returning to that great black ship in the lagoon. Images of unknown figures, more demon than men, played in his mind. He drove those ideas out again and again and was ashamed of his own fear.

A thought occurred to Linot. He was trusting Mundan to know where to look for the island, and was trusting his old eyes to see far enough to spot it. What if the old man missed it? Is it possible that with all his preoccupation with chants and spells Mundan had forgotten the one real thing he knew: navigation? And if he had, what could Linot do about it? He fretted about this new concern, pondering and discarding various solutions. He resolved to question Mundan, in hopes of discerning the truth. As soon as he had a stringer of fish Linot climbed out of the pool and headed for the canoe. There was no sign of Mundan on any of the high points. Linot wondered why the old man was wandering so aimlessly. He frowned, wondering if the old fool was wasting time by making prayers to placate the "island spirits" as he wandered. Impatience drove the anxiety from his belly and Linot was again resentful that he was burdened with the old man. Linot spotted a furtive figure moving through the rocks near the boat, and decided to check in with his older partner.

"Old man," Linot called, hopping from boulder to boulder, heading toward the canoe. The figure ducked down out of sight in the broken rock at the beach's edge. "Mundan," Linot called, correcting the early impudence of his address. "What did you see?" There was no reply, but Linot again caught a glimpse of movement in the rocks ahead. Anger flared in Linot's heart at the old fool's odd ways. He scrambled awkwardly across the jagged boulders of coral, his thoughts vacillating between a proper patience with the elderly and giving the old wanderer a proper tongue-lashing. "Mundan!" he called again. He thought he heard a reply, but the crash of waves erased any meaning. He climbed laboriously over a dozen more big blocks of coral and then Linot was at the edge of an overhang, looking down at the beach. Only the boat was there. Footprints in the sand wove between small rocks and vanished under the cliff edge. Try as he would, leaning over the edge, Linot could not see under the overhang. "Mundan!" No answer. He studied the beach, and picked out a patch of sand with no rocks. Linot gathered himself up and jumped down, tumbling onto his face. He picked himself up and spat out the sand, fuming. He turned back toward the cliff. "Old man, what ..."

There was a shallow cave hollowed out under the coral overhang, and the person Linot was following was waiting there, but it was not Mundan. It was no person Linot had ever seen. Indeed, he barely saw the person, or thing, at all. It was dark, and tall, and very fast, and almost human. Blue scales covered the torso and limbs, and talons terminated the long fingers. It hissed loudly, shocking Linot, who stumbled backwards. The creature leaped past him towards the sea. As it passed it slammed into Linot, spinning him around and knocking him down. He landed belly-down on hard coral, enduring insult and injury of the most outrageous sort. His fear drove him back to his feet, but by the time he could get up the beast was gone, with only churning water to mark its passing. Linot ran mindlessly away across the beach, away from the water. He leaped up into the rocks, headless of the knife-edges of stone. He stopped once he was up off the sand, looking back at the water's edge. He could see nothing but waves. Hearing a sound behind he spun about, but this time it was indeed Mundan.

"What is it?" Mundan asked.

"We must go!" Linot shouted, and turned back toward the boat. Just beyond the dugout, with its promise of familiar safety and escape, lay the deep and mysterious ocean. Linot hesitated, then leaped down onto the sand. He ran to the boat and seized the hull. Mundan was not far behind him. "What did you see!?!", demanded Mundan, but Linot was all business. "Just go!" he shouted, and together they shoved the canoe back into the water and paddled it away. It was not until they were bobbing up and down in deep water that Linot's heart slowed to normal.

"What did you see?" Mundan demanded, staring at the younger man. He scowled. "Did you meet an island spirit?"

"No! No!" Linot shouted. He looked down, and was startled to see his own knife clenched tightly in his fist. He had no memory of drawing it. He looked back up to find Mundan staring fiercely at him. "No, I --- " His words failed him. "Yes. Yes, I --- I saw something."

Mundan looked around the boat into the deep blue around them. He withdrew a leather pouch from around his neck, one of the few items he wore. He shook the contents into the water and chanted a spell. Linot watched, wide-eyed, alternating between Mundan's enchantment and the dark water around. Then Mundan seized a paddle, and Linot followed suit. Together they laid to. The small island fell behind and disappeared behind the swells. They did not talk, and they did not even pause until Linot's throat was burning of thirst and he had to reach for his water gourd. The cuts he received from the rocks still bled, and stung when sweat rolled into them. Linot replayed the encounter again and again and again in his mind's eye, and the terror of this drove his arms until they ached. The two did not stop rowing until a tell-tale cloud appeared in the sky ahead, the sign of an island. After what seemed like both a lifetime and a moment, Nemdahod appeared.

The sight of the familiar shoreline did not bring the relief Linot expected. Dozens of shoals, hundreds of waves, and thousands of oar strokes lay between them and home. Every wave potentially concealed a mystery, a threat. Linot tried to explain to himself what he had seen, and could not. Eventually the waves were cresting on rocks around them, and they were heading in through the channel. Finally, the calm waters of the lagoon greeted them and relief swept over Linot as they glided past the familiar landmarks. Then Linot looked down into the depths of the lagoon, and the memory of that horror reappeared in his mind. He envisioned it rising even from these familiar waters, to seize and rend, and his feet ached for land. As they passed the foreign ship with its oddly colored crew, Mundan made the sign to ward off the evil eye. Linot stared at the older man for a long moment, then made the same sign himself.

CHAPTER TWO

The Island

Petron woke because there was a foot in his face. It was a small foot, and placed without malice, for the owner thereof was still asleep himself, tucked under Petron's left side. It was Bighair, one of the village boys. He had managed to get himself flipped end over end, and one of his feet was under Petron's nose. This was not an unusual way for Petron to wake up on the island. He gently pushed the foot away. Bighair twisted a bit and pulled his legs in but did not awaken. Petron gathered his thoughts in the dark, feeling the moist tropical air waft in under the woven wall of the giant grass hut that had become his home. It took just a moment for his reality to come back to him. He was a sailor. He was marooned. No one here spoke his language, no one was coming for him, and he had no way off the island.

He hadn't been on the island terribly long before the village children adopted him as one of their own. This was not surprising since most of the adults treated him as if he were a child, most likely because of his inability to speak their language. Indeed, in this strange land with its strange ways, almost any child older than eight was more useful than Petron when it came to doing chores. Not that there were many chores -- life on the island was simple. Petron lay there, unmoving, waiting for the child at his side to wake up. The sun was still hidden beyond the horizon, but outside of the great house some of the wives would already be stirring, preparing to light the great fire for the day. Soon the men would be looking for food and then prepare to set sail in their long boats, off to fish for yet another day. Petron would join the children and older men in casting the fine nets into the shallower waters, work more suited for the weak of body or feeble of mind, or tongue. It was humbling, for sure, but it was a place to be.

How long had he been there? He wasn't sure. Seven days? Nine? He had lost count, and there was no one who cared to remind him. No one had much cared where he came from, or what his plans were. As a village, they had taken him into their great house, and as a village they had shown him how to fish with the nets. It was as if they expected to find mute men stranded on their shores occasionally. And perhaps they did. Petron was glad that they hadn't killed and eaten him, as he had heard tales of. He was new to life on the sea, but the journey south had been a long one and there had been many a hour to fill with stories and songs.

Hardly a minute went by before Bighair stirred. Petron pushed the child gently out of his hammock and got up himself. They were in an untidy corner of the great house, behind where the lesser families slept. While the little one stretched and moaned, Petron tied on his belt. Like all the locals, Petron used the belt to carry a knife. Also, like the locals, it was his only item of clothing. He still hadn't figured out where the rest of his clothes had gone. Indeed, he still hadn't figured out where "here" was.

He remembered the terror of the storm, the despair of being cast alone into the deep, and then awakening to see dark curious faces peering down at him. He did not understand their speech, nor they his. They accepted him as he was, though, and so he didn't worry about the whereabouts of his trousers. With his belt firmly in place, Petron walked through the great house towards the nearest door. Many of the villagers were already up, but many also still lay in their hammocks with spouses, friends or assorted children.

He walked to the latrine to relieve himself, pausing a moment to touch the totem at the door as he had been taught. Bighair had followed him out to the latrine and made his own contribution to the collection of urine in the great collecting basin. This done, the two stepped out of the rough hut to find another village child awaiting them. This was Temma. Bighair and Temma seemed to be Petron's designated escorts. Petron wasn't sure of their ages. The villagers tended to be a shorter race and both children followed that trend. Petron guessed that Bighair was about twelve and Temma was about ten. Bighair had earned his name by his habit of tousling his hair into a puffy mess throughout the day. What his actual name was Petron was not entirely sure. On the other hand, Petron was fairly sure that he had Temma's name right, for her mother often called for her, sending the little girl running obediently home for some chore or other.

With the morning ritual done, Petron grabbed his nets and headed right down to the water, his matched pair of small locals in tow. They had been teaching him the right fish to catch, and he had been teaching them various ways to mend the nets. Together they had been learning the right places to go to find the best fish. While Bighair and Petron went straight to the water, Temma detoured past the great fire and fetched some breakfast for the trio: dried fish and roasted root. Petron ate sparingly. The fish was pleasant enough, but the root just wasn't to his taste. As they ate, Petron explained to them how the nets were made. He was sure they didn't understand him, but he told them anyway.

This morning the fishing was good. Petron had been doing it for several days now and had only caught small fish. But this morning he and the two kids pulled in several larger fish in addition to the usual batch of small fish. He let Temma thread them onto a twine and keep them while he and Bighair brought in the smaller ones. Once the smaller fish were safely contained, Petron swapped jobs with Temma; he took the bigger fish and let her and Bighair take in the smaller fish. The two children dragged the net with the smaller fish off to the village, and Petron followed along with his string of fish. When they headed down to the great fire, he instead looked around for a good place to gut his catch. Spotting a set of benches in the shade of a canopy of trees, Petron decided one of the benches would make a good work table, laid the fish out atop it, and set to work cleaning his catch.

Petron had just about finished when he noticed one of the village women coming toward him. She had a distressed look on her face. She came up within a dozen feet of him and then stood there, pointing at him and talking. She seemed agitated about something, but he understood none of what she was saying. He listened for a moment, then got up to go, assuming his absence would improve matters. He hadn't gone more than a few feet when she suddenly started jabbering even louder and moved to block him. The sound of her words brought other women over. Petron tried to leave, but she blocked him again and was joined in her efforts by another woman. After a minute or so of their pointing and yelling it occurred to Petron that they were pointing at the fish guts he had laid on the ground beside the bench. It occurred to him that perhaps the women were offended by the innards, and so he scooped them up and moved to take them away. Improbably, this seemed to somehow make matters even worse. The women began to scream and shake their hands at him and slap their bare chests. Some even fell to their knees crying. Petron stood there paralyzed, totally at a loss for what to do. It was as if all the women had suddenly gone insane. Even the children had crowded around, weeping and wringing their hands.

The commotion drew the attention of one of the men, and he was now striding purposefully towards the crowd. Petron felt a sense of relief, at least in part because the man was not running, but was just walking purposefully forward. As he approached Petron held up his bloody burden and shrugged his shoulders, to show his confusion, but the man just glanced at Petron. He looked instead over Petron's head, at something behind Petron. Coming straight on, the man simultaneously slapped the fish guts from Petron's hands and gave Petron a hard shove that sent him to the ground. Petron was so startled he just lay there. The man scooped up the innards and carefully arranged them on a small bench, just to the side of where Petron had been sitting. Petron watched, dumbfounded. The man remained in a bowed posture for a long moment, saying something, and then the crowd of women echoed his words and he stood. He approached Petron with a hand extended and lifted Petron quickly to his feet. Petron was about to thank the man when the man promptly grabbed him by the elbow and roughly propelled him away from the area. They cleared the circle of women and the man released him with a small shove, motioning him away dismissively. Petron stood there, absolutely confused. The man started walking away, looking back over his shoulder and saying something in a calm but annoyed tone and shooing Petron away. He said something to the women, and they all walked back to the huts, leaving Petron totally befuddled. For a long time, Petron stood there, indignation warring with fear and confusion in his head. What had just happened? He wasn't sure what to do. Should he leave? To go where? What should he do now? The crisis appeared to have passed, but what had the crisis been in the first place?

While he stood there, he noticed a small figure detach itself from the shadows around the huts and move towards him. It was Bighair. The boy walked up to the spot that Petron had been sitting. He took the last fish, the one Petron hadn't finished cleaning, and deftly gutted it. He laid the entrails with the others and made a small bow towards the bloody pile. He then took the cleaned fish and Petron's knife and carried them over to Petron. He handed Petron the knife, said something with a shrug, and walked back towards the huts with the fish.

Petron watched the lad go. The beginnings of understanding were growing in his mind. He stared at the small arrangement of benches where the incident occurred. He could see now that it was actually a small pavilion. Where the entrails had been laid, there was a small wall or trellis erected. Being careful not to trespass any closer than the women had, he moved around for a better view. It was difficult to see into the shadows. Petron had not had any reason to investigate this spot before and had never noticed it, but now he could see that there were things up in the canopy, suspended from the trees. Petron squinted against the glare of bright daylight on white sand. Those things were sharks. Most were small, but one was large enough to be menacing, even dead and dry as these were. Petron could feel goose-flesh on his arms. The sharks had been skinned and stuffed and hung from the trees. The large one was as long as he was tall. Its mouth gaped wide, a toothy rictus of death. For the first time in days, Petron felt naked, his exposed balls shriveling despite the heat. He stared a moment longer, expecting to see more, and was not disappointed. Above the sharks, forming a sort of cap over the pavillion, there was suspended a spirit face.

A life at sea was filled with routine, and terror. On the ocean, mysteries abound. Petron had learned early to accept that there were times and places and circumstances he would not be able to control, and he had learned to control his fear. He remembered the first time he had seen a Slith. He had heard of the strange race, and had been warned of how alien they were. Many had whispered that they were humans once, warped and changed by a dark god. Petron did not believe that, and he felt that he had managed the encounter well. Nonetheless, the sight of the strange person, with their unnaturally large eyes and their hair of feathers, had startled him, regardless of his external calm, and had haunted his dreams. Seeing the sharks arranged above him, with the spirit face over all them, rekindled that internal panic, that feeling that there were fey spirits just out of sight. He stood, unmoving, forcing himself to see it all, and to control his emotions.

It was at that moment that Petron felt eyes on him. He turned around, and there, standing several paces behind him stood an old woman. Petron recognized her as the village healer. She held a large bag woven of fronds and was staring intently at him, frowning. She said something to him, which he did not understand. Petron shook his head. She repeated herself, louder, as if by raising her voice she would be more comprehensible. Petron again shook his head and shrugged. She made a clicking noise with her tongue, shaking her head in disgust. She bent down and took some sand up in her hand, leaving the bag on the ground. She slowly straightened and started chanting in a strange, high-pitched tone of voice. Petron looked around, but there was no one else there to help him with the old woman. She had a leather pouch tied around her neck on a cord, and she now took this pouch and tapped it against the handful of sand. She then suddenly flung the sand at Petron. Even though she was at least five paces away, he suddenly felt the grit in his eyes. Petron staggered, reeling. He turned away from her, wiping at his eyes, and staggering away. When he could finally open his eyes again, she was gone, completely out of sight, even though he had closed his eyes for only a dozen heartbeats. Feeling suddenly lost, Petron took his bloody blade and walked away up the beach, away from the village.

Not for the first time, Petron considered how he could get off the island. It was unlikely anyone from his ship would be looking for him; he was almost certainly written off as lost at sea. If he was to ever get back to his home in the colder north, he would have to do it himself. The question was how. Almost as soon as he had seen the men pushing the long boats into the water Petron knew that he would have to secure a place in one of those boats. He had tried, the first few days he was on the island, but had been rudely driven away. He considered making his own boat, but he had no experience making boats. Petron had resigned himself to learning the language well enough to ask for passage.

A day passed since the incident with the fish guts with no other great incidents, and things quickly settled back into a routine. Petron was sitting on a small woven stool in the shade of one of the few trees around, cleaning his last catch of the day. He couldn't help but notice that most of the men and many of the women were gathered around the great fire. Petron could hear animated conversation. He wasn't quite sure about what, but he did notice that after the incident at the shark altar he seemed to have picked up a few of the local words. He sat and listened, trying to piece together the gist.

After a while, Temma walked up to him and motioned him to follow her. Petron did, and she led him to the group. When they arrived, they found a circle of men seated in the center of a large group of women and children. Temma's father motioned Petron to sit at his side. Petron did, and Temma's father proceeded to launch into a long speech that seemed to be about Petron. At the end, Temma's father pointed at Temma and motioned her forward. He started talking again, this time pointing at Petron and Temma. After a few moments, various of the men began to nod in agreement. They all then looked at Petron. He looked back at them, and then shrugged and shook his head in confusion. Everyone just laughed. Temma's father said a few words, and everyone got up and headed off to their various places, leaving Petron and Temma and her father. Petron stood as the man approached, but he ignored Petron and spoke instead to the girl, speaking confidently to her, then patting Petron familiarly on the shoulder and walking away. Petron stood there with Temma, alone. She looked up at him and said something slowly and confidently to him, which he did not understand. She then surprised him by saying, rather understandably, "come on," gesturing for him to follow and walked toward the great hut. It was then that Petron knew what had happened: he had been given a nanny.

The next day started the same, with a small, smelly person sharing his hammock. Now, however, it was Temma, not Bighair, whose foot was in his face. He gently plopped her out onto the floor and unwrapped himself. A quick stretch, a wrapping on of the belt, and they were out for the day. Temma did not leave his side but followed him, talking and pointing the while. When he stopped in the latrine, she followed him in and just stood and waited, still talking and pointing at things. There was only one latrine, and he had gotten used to the women and girls being in it with him, but he was not used to this much attention. He shooed her away, but she shook her head, still talking. Now she was pointing at him. Petron shrugged and took aim. For a long moment, nothing was happening: Petron was not used to a running commentary on his performance. Then the casualness of it struck him, and the day began to flow again.

His business done, Petron left the latrine, Temma in tow. Bighair appeared from the great house, they all got some food, and they headed for the water. Soon he and the two children were fishing again just like the day before, albeit with more talking. Petron finally realized that she was teaching him her language, and so he started teaching her his. She would point at random things and say something, and he would respond with his own names for them. The day went by quickly, and from that day on Temma was almost always by his side. No longer did her mother call her away, and from then on she slept with him, ate with him, fished with him, and walked with him. And the whole time she talked. She talked and talked and pointed and gesticulated and touched things and herself and even him.

Several days later, at evening time, Petron took a walk up the hill. The village was set on a beach with a wasteland of scrub brush behind it. There were trails leading inland through the brush, and not too far from the village, the land rose to a peak. It occurred to Petron that from that peak he might be able to see any other islands in the area, so he struck off toward it through the thickets, Temma in tow. As they walked Temma chattered on, pointing and waving her arms and touching everything. Petron was starting to understand the cadence of the language, and was happy to learn, and teach. Soon he had taught her the words for bushes, and trees, and the sky, and hands and feet and eyes and the path and walking and running. He realized that she had a child's natural knack for learning, something he no longer had. He concentrated his effort on helping her learn his language.

As they climbed higher and higher Petron would find vantage points to mount: boulders and outcroppings and even tree stumps. Gradually he was seeing the layout of the island. As he learned the layout he grew more and more appreciative of the durability of the natives. The island was almost all scrub. As they walked and occasionally ran, Petron and Temma came across a fair number of large tree stumps, but very few large trees. Many of the tree stumps were charred, but not all. Petron considered what he had eaten on the island. Except for the roots and some greens, he didn't recall much in the way of non-meat food at all. Another thing Petron soon noticed, even in the growing dimness, was that in several places the water around the island grew deep fast. Petron knew that heavy seas liked deep water, and he wondered fearfully when the storm season was. He hoped not to be on the island when it hit.

As the pair walked higher and higher Petron noticed that Temma talked less. The sun was lowering on the horizon, and the sky was growing darker. There could be no large animals on an island so small, Petron reasoned, but he expected that his young tutor had little experience being so far from home. Finally, he stopped climbing and just looked around. He saw no ships, and no other islands, although he saw some clouds on the horizon that could have marked one. After a good look around, he let Temma lead him back down the hill.

Dawn found Petron already awake, thinking of the boats and how to get a ride off the island. He went to the shore, as was his new routine, and threw the nets with the two children. As they fished, Petron stole glances at the men preparing the boats for the daily fishing trip. He wondered how long the village could survive without the fish caught each day. He suspected not long. He also wondered how far out the fishermen ventured, and if they traded with the other islands. He hoped to ride out with them as soon as possible. Petron was not the only one watching the boats, either. Bighair watched them prepare as well. Petron thought him too small yet for the boats, but Petron could see at least one boy on the boats that was not a lot older. Considering the scars and injuries Petron had seen on some of the fishermen, the use of such young boys on the boats surprised Petron. As the boats launched, Bighair ran out as far into the water as possible, shouting to the men on the boats. Petron assumed he was wishing them well. Only when the boats were well away did Bighair return to his nets.

The tides lent a natural rhythm to the day. Petron, like the few older men of the village, fished while the tide was high and the shallows were flooded. As the waters ebbed he and the two children followed the waters out until the steepening drop-off threatened. When the waves grew too rough and close to handle the nets he would retreat. The other men would nap, along with the women and kids. Petron took that time to explore. Previously Temma and Bighair had napped with their families, but now Temma followed him. Together they hiked out into the brush, pointing at things as they went. Temma remembered many of the words from the previous day, but Petron was still rather lost. It was obvious to him that she would have to be his translator. He just hoped he could pick up enough words to go out with the boatmen soon.

They hadn't gone too far when Petron noticed the stone block. It was rather obvious, as it was lying right in the center of a footpath. In fact, the footpath split and passed equally to either side of it. Temma hopped up on it as she passed. Petron immediately noticed how regular it was, and realized that it had been cut. There seemed to be some sort of markings on it, but he could not make them out. They continued on, and Temma took the lead, picking her way through various forks in the road until the path petered out in an area of thinner undergrowth. While Petron watched, she gave him a small dissertation that seemed to be centered on something that the villages came to this spot for, then she got down on her hands and knees and started digging. In a short while, she had unearthed a root like the ones the villagers ate. Petron looked around him. There were no obvious signs of cultivation here, but he could see that people had been digging there for a while. Having gotten one root, Temma quickly unearthed a few more. That done, she handed a few to him, and then led the duo back to the village with their cargo.

Back at the village, the locals were up from their naps and milling about, preparing to get back to the business of the day. Temma carried her tuberous treasure to the great hut, where her mother was flaying fish. Petron also handed the woman his roots. As he did so, he noticed that she sported many fine lines drawn across her flanks. He hadn't noticed these on any of the other villagers before. He didn't want to be seen to be staring, but when the mother turned away to store the roots he got a good look. The lines seemed to be drawings of fish scales. He filed that away in his mind for future reference.

Fishing resumed with the return of the tide and continued until the return of the fishing boats. Bighair ran off to join the villagers in welcoming back the men and to see what they had caught. An interesting variety of fish was unloaded. Petron noted that one man was injured, apparently on his shoulder, and was taken aside by an older woman to have his wounds tended. Petron watched them walk up the beach, wondering how a man could get such a wound on a fishing trip, but decided that was one more island mystery that would have to wait. With fish in tow, the village retired to the great fire for supper. When the eating turned to singing, Petron and Temma slipped away and headed back up the hill. This time they made better time and stayed to watch the sun touch the horizon. They arrived back at the village just in time to join Bighair in Petron's hammock for bedtime.

The nets that the island people used were woven of thread that they made from a local weed. Petron quickly learned how they broke apart the stems and twined the threads together. It wasn't the strongest fiber Petron had ever used -- if he could find his own shirt he could unravel it for better -- but it was serviceable. The nets required constant repair, and thus it was that Petron was sitting in the shade of the great house with Temma and a heap of dried weeds, repairing nets. Together they were working to entwine the fibers into thread and tie the thread into the net to fix the tears.

It was as they were working that Petron suddenly felt a sharp pain in his backside. It felt like he had suddenly been poked with a red-hot poker. He leaped to his feet, his hand on the offended spot. To his horror, there was something stuck to his bottom, and it was moving. He ripped it away and flung it on the ground, dancing away. It was a large black insect of some sort, or crab perhaps, and as he watched it rapidly buried itself in the sand. Temma had already come to her feet, and she was on it in a flash, stomping it until it was a damp, flattened smear. Petron looked at his hand, and it was bloodied. He could feel blood running down his right leg now. Temma came and looked at the injury, which Petron himself was having a hard time seeing, due to its location. Temma said something in a worried hushed tone, then ran away.

"Temma," Petron said, starting after her, but to his surprise his right leg folded under him and he fell to the sand. It felt as if someone was stabbing him there still, almost as if there were a spine still stuck in the wound. He pressed his hand against the spot, probing, but there was only the wound, which was now throbbing. Petron looked about for more of the accursed pests, but there were none, something he was grateful for. He got up, favoring the injured leg. Petron pressed his hand against the wound to stop the bleeding and was worried when it would not stop. Now he could see Temma running back to him from a small hut set off from the great hut.

"Come you on," she said, waving to him, then turned back towards the far-off hut. "Come you on."

She had picked up many of his words quite quickly, mostly the ones he used on her. He obediently arose and began to limp after her, following her across the hot dry sand to the hut. He had seen this hut many times; it was the hut of the village healer. It was smaller than the great hut and cluttered with all sorts of totems and fetishes. There was even a slab of rock by the door that had a small spirit face carved into it. Of all the locals, the healer was the only one who seemed to own any clothing. She could sometimes be seen wearing a large shawl made of woven fronds and a straw hat. He had mostly avoided her, as she seemed a somewhat erratic person, prone to sudden fits of speech. He, of course, could understand none of what she said, and he suspected that in truth none of the villagers could either.

Petron entered the hut and stopped. He stood in the door, peering about, feeling the throbbing from his leg. As his eyes adjusted, he could see several of the village women also seated around. He was in a room that seemed to take up less than half the hut. At the back of the hut was a wall with a small round door, through which peered several young female faces. As he looked back at their curious gaze it occurred to him that he hadn't seen many teen girls in the village. Now he knew why -- they were all in here. How that happened, he didn't know.

The healer approached him, her hands caked with some sort of colorful mud. She waved and pointed up at the roof and chattered at Temma, who seemed to be considering her words.

"Please up roof you hands," Temma said.

"Tacho?" Petron replied, using one of the few words he did know. It meant "what?" He tried to keep the impatience and panic from his voice. His leg was going numb.

Temma mimed for him, as she spoke. "Up roof hands, you up hands, roof, please."

Petron hesitantly lifted his hands up to the roof, looking askance at Temma. She nodded, then shook her head. "Here," she said, stepping over to the center post of the hut. She pointed up at one of the poles that supported the roof, and she jumped up a bit, looking at him. He hobbled over to the spot and reached up, taking hold of the pole. He could feel the eyes of all the women on him. Temma hopped up and down, saying "up" over and over again. He pushed up, but the pole didn't move. Then he pulled up, lifting himself off the ground, and Temma nodded and smiled. When he did that, his right leg suddenly convulsed, flopping wildly. That frightened Petron and the women collectively muttered and sighed. Fear seized Petron's chest, but the old healer just nattered dismissively at the others. She stepped up to Petron and held up her hands coated with the blue mud, then stepped around behind him and planted both her hands squarely and loudly on his backside.

When she did this it felt like her hands were made of hot steel, and Petron yelped and tried to pull himself up and away. His right leg flopped around again and he hissed in agony. He kept his grip, though, expecting this was somehow therapy for the bite. The old woman turned away to a large pot and plunged her hands in. She yammered something and the other women got up and joined her at the pot. One of them brought a tall jug and poured some liquid in, and another dumped in some powder from a sack. They all plunged in their hands and kneaded the mix. Petron's arms grew tired and he eased himself down. His right leg felt like it had fallen asleep and was just now waking. Still, the pain was lessening, and he was feeling a bit safer. The old woman came back, her hands now coated with red. She barked a command, and Temma and another woman cleared away the various stools and sacks and things from where he was balanced precariously on one leg. Then the woman seized a large jar and splashed cold water on his backside. She and Temma began to wash off the mud the healer had put on. Temma got the right side, he could tell from her lighter touch, but every time she touched the wound he wanted to squeal with pain.

Once the initial application was gone the healer motioned upwards, and Temma said "up" again. Petron hauled himself up off his feet, and all the women swarmed in around him, smearing him with the red paste from his armpits downward. The paste had a heady aroma, redolent of alcohol and spice. Almost immediately he could feel his strength fading, and simultaneously his arms locked in place. It was as if he couldn't move, but he would soon lose his grip and fall. Meanwhile, a dozen hands were swiping and slapping and wiping and smearing every inch of his dangling body. Not normally a ticklish person, he found himself twitching and lurching at the invasions, especially when they treated his loins, an event that he felt happened far more often than it needed to. He could hear his heart beating louder, and could feel the blood rushing to his head. It felt like his eyes were swelling shut. His strength was gone now, and he could not even feel the rest of his body, but he could not let go. Now the hands, disembodied like ghosts, stopped their motion and just attached themselves to him, pressing harder and harder, crushing him. The fumes were overpowering him. He couldn't see. The hands were shaking him, pulling him sideways. Night closed over him, as he heard Temma saying, over and over, "let go." Finally, he let go, and the world closed shut.

Petron was already watching the woman as she watched him before he realized he was awake again. He was lying down on the floor of a hut. She was standing there, one hand on the center pole of the hut, staring intently at him, and he didn't know what she wanted. Then he saw the girl. The girl was kneeling beside the woman, facing her, touching her on the leg. That's Temma, his brain told him. Oh, another part of his brain replied. And that's her mother, the first part said. Petron decided this was all too complex, and closed his eyes again.

Later, when he opened his eyes again, his leg hurt. He wasn't sure which one hurt, but it hurt. In fact, his back hurt too, and his arms, and his balls, and his belly. Even his jaws hurt. He tried to rise, but that proved to be a very hard thing to manage. He was so heavy. His skin felt thick. That woman was still there, and so was Temma. She was still staring at him, and Temma was still kneeling, drawing on the woman's leg. Petron realized that the woman was Temma's mother. She was tall, and very broad, even for a native. The old healer was there too, walking around the two and muttering and touching Temma's mother. After a bit, Petron realized that the old woman was also drawing on Temma's mother, who was covered in a webbing of fine black lines. Temma's mother could not take her eyes off him, the expression on her face almost like hunger. She said something, half smiling, and Temma looked up at her, then over at Petron. Temma smiled and came to Petron's side.

"Petron," she said and kissed him. Petron suddenly felt flooded with a terribly unexpected emotion -- gratitude for the girl's love. He tried to rise, but Temma put her hand on his forehead and held him down. He was surprised at how strong she was suddenly. When she removed her hand, he looked down at his too-heavy body and saw that it was caked with the red mud, which had been swirled and sketched on his body in arcane runes, and which was now cracking and falling off. His head started to buzz, and the world started to tilt. He lay back again. Temma leaned over him and put her hand on his face. She said something, but he didn't understand what.

The sunlight was orange when he woke up again. He felt weak and woozy and even a bit nauseated, but he was so stiff he had to move. He also had to pee like mad. He sat up, then waited for his vision to return and for the world to stop moving. When his eyesight cleared, he saw Temma beside him and the old healer sitting in front of him. She said something, slowly and clearly. He didn't quite understand the words, but the tone and attitude seemed comforting and affirming as if she was saying he would be all right. He nodded. Temma helped him as he stood. His right leg was still quite weak, and Temma handed him a big cane. He limped outside, squinting in the sunlight. The day was almost over now. Villagers milled about in their usual post-dinner languor. The healer was at his side, and Temma, and the healer instructed Temma. Pointing at Petron and making walking motions with her hand, Temma nodded and looked at Petron.

"You walk please, much, please," she said.

Petron nodded, understanding that some exercise was therapeutic now. He limped towards the brush. He caught sight of Temma's father near the fire pit. Their eyes met for a moment, then the other man nodded and moved on. Petron and Temma made their slow way towards the scrub, Petron shedding flakes of red as he moved, Temma slowly and carefully explaining as best she could that walking was good. He paused at the first big bush to relieve himself, not even considering waiting until he could reach the latrine. He then followed Temma as she led him along the trails. Sure enough, as he walked he could feel his strength returning. His leg ached, and there was a sore spot on his rear where that thing had bitten him. He was just glad it had picked his broad backside and not something smaller and more tender.

Petron's whole body was trembling with weakness as he limped along. He was grateful the natives had a medicine for the bug bite, and that he had been in the village when he got bit. He wondered how many men hadn't been so lucky, and how many survived their greater misfortune. As he walked Petron also wondered where the healer had accumulated her many potions and drugs. How many did she have, that she had just the right antidote for the thing that afflicted him? Were these things so common that she just had the treatment handy? Or was there some magic that she applied to make a common cure fit an uncommon malady? And what was the meaning of the lines on Temma's mother? None of the other women in the village wore them. And as for how she looked at him, he didn't need to ask what that meant. He had not seen that look often, but he knew it. Petron worried that the woman might try to act on the feelings behind that look. That was not the sort of trouble Petron needed to court.

Temma proved to be a stubborn taskmaster. She led Petron up and down the trails as the sun set. Apparently, she had been given the command to make him walk, but had not been told when to quit. Finally, they ended up in the yam patch and Petron sat down on a block of stone in protest. Temma scolded him for a bit, then wandered off. As he rested, Petron carefully scanned the ground around for more of those black beasts. He saw none. He did see many of the stone blocks, though, and he quickly realized that they were laid out in lines. After a bit of rest, he stood and wandered among the field of blocks. Tracing them, he came to see that they seemed to form into rectangles. Here and there he spotted chunks of burned wood, and he realized that the blocks had once been buildings, which had burned down.

Some of the blocks further afield were still stacked one atop another. Petron got up and hobbled over to look at them. He stooped and looked at the carvings on their sides -- markings that looked like people and boats and fish. The symbol for the shark figured prominently. He climbed atop the blocks and looked about. There were enough foundations for a village. He could also see Temma returning for him, carrying food and water. He sat down on the stones and let her bring him the tucker, eating and sharing with her. When he was done, she lay her head in his lap and held his hand. He patted her on her head, then together they walked back to the village.

The next day Petron stood in the shallows and watched the boats go out to sea. He studied their clean lines and took note of the way the men handled the oars. He knew that the only way off the island was by water, and he needed to be ready to take the opportunity to go when it arose. His leg still hurt from the previous day's incident, and his skill in the local tongue was still very poor, so he knew that he would need to work harder on learning the basic words. It would no longer be good enough for Temma to translate for him -- he needed to start speaking for himself.

"Temma," he said. She looked up from her net. He held up the net and said "Apa ini," which he understood to mean "what do you call this?" Temma knew this game and had great patience with it.

"Bersih," she replied. "Net."

Petron pointed out at the boats. "Apa ini?"

"Perahu. Boats."

Petron then leaned down and splashed his hand through the water. "Apa ini?"

"Otas. Water."

He opened his mouth for the next word, then paused, momentarily lost. He was standing naked in the middle of the ocean, net fishing, and he had just asked the words for "net", "boats", and "water". He was out of words. The pause lasted only a moment, though. As he held up his hand. "Apa ini?"

"Lengan. Hand."

"Lengan," he repeated. "Apa ini?" he asked, tapping his thigh as he cast his net.

"Kaki. Leg."

"Kaki. Apa ini?" he patted his stomach.

"Perut. belly."

"Perut. Apa ini?" He thumped his chest.

"Dada. Chest."

"Apa ini?" he asked, patting his head.

"Rambut. Hair."

"No, I ... never mind. Apa ini?" he asked, taking his head in his hand and rolling it a bit.

"Kepala. Head."

"Kepala." Thinking of heads of hair, he pointed at Bighair, who was staring out after the boats, his neglected net drifting in the swells. "Apa ini?"

"Kotujo. Bighair."

"No, well, yes," he said. Petron had recently learned that "Kotujo" was Bighair's real name, but that wasn't the word Petron was looking for. He was looking for the word for "boy". He hesitated, embarrassed, trying to figure out a polite way to indicate gender, then gave up and tapped his own groin, then pointed at Bighair, then pointed at her groin and shook his head, then pointed at himself and Bighair a few times rapidly. "Apa ini?" he asked, tossing out his net.

Temma cocked her head to one side, a blank look on her face. Petron felt his face flush, but then she nodded. "Laki laki," Temma said, then paused. Petron filled in the word: "boy." She pointed to herself, with a quick gesture towards her own loins, then said, "Gadis."

"Girl. Laki laki, gadis," Petron repeated, then touched the knife slung on his belt. "Apa ini?"

"Pisau. Knife."

"Pisau," Petron said, pulling in the net. He could feel some resistance this time. He pulled up a middling fish. "Aha!" he called, seizing the wriggling catch. "Apa ini?"

"Makanan," Temma replied, coming toward him with the holding rope. "Supper."

The language lesson continued throughout the day. When the villagers took a break for the noonday nap, Petron and Temma took a tour of the village, pointing out things. In the afternoon, as they fished, they practiced some common sayings and polite salutations. By the evening both were growing weary of the task. After supper Temma stayed close to her family hut, playing with the other children. Petron hiked back out into the scrub, to where he had seen the ruins the day before. He wandered around in the scrub for a while, allowing his thoughts to drift, replaying the words and phrases over in his mind. He noted the layout of the foundations, recognizing streets and alleys. More than once he found various artifacts lying half-buried in the sand. Some he recognized as household goods, or tools, or even weapons. Some of them were strange, looking like they came from a different place, while others could easily have come from the village that very day. Many were burned.

As the sun set Petron lay down on a line of stones, his head awhirl. There was so much to learn. He did not feel anywhere near ready to tackle the task of asking for a ride off the island,

and yet he felt lonelier now than he had in a week. He needed to be home in Braemond. Even the sound of the insects in the brush was wrong. As he lay there, the sound of voices caught his ear. He rolled a lazy head to see who was coming. It seemed that in his wanderings he had circled back around to one of the paths. At first, he could see nothing, and then a hint of movement could be discerned through the brush. Figures drew near. Petron couldn't make out faces through the leaves, so he shifted himself until he had a better view. The interlopers consisted of three women and a man.

The four people were chatting and laughing happily, their speech far too fast for Petron to follow. He realized that Temma had been speaking slowly for him for quite a while. They stopped not far away, and the women stooped and dug. Petron realized that his meanderings had led him back to where Temma had first brought him. The women handed the tubers up to the man, who was carrying a basket. Their mood was high, and they were laughing and chatting in teasing voices. Some of the tubers ended up tossed at the man, who had to catch them while balancing the basket with one hand. More than once he got a playful slap on the behind, which he only half-heartedly tried to dodge. Petron felt no need to stand and identify himself. Hidden behind the screen of brush, he could observe invisibly. Petron felt no obligation to rise and help. He had no objection to work -- he could watch people do it all day in fact.

The natives, none of whom he could definitively place or name, were as industrious as they were giddy. The basket filled quickly. Finally, the women stood up and stretched. One put her hands on the basket the young man was carrying and pushed down, talking loudly. He protested good-naturedly, and the other woman put her hands on his shoulders and jumped up onto his back, her legs straddling his hips. He almost collapsed, but still managed to keep his grip on the basket. She jumped off, laughing, and the others all laughed as well. Petron felt their reflected good humor, and almost chuckled himself. It was good to watch the happy interplay, even from the shadows. The two women then started walking back towards the village, leaning on each other and calling back as they faded into the distance.

The man stayed, still holding the heavy basket. The remaining woman watched the other two women walk away, then turned to talk to the man. With a shock, Petron recognized her as Temma's mother. She knelt again, digging, and he stood with the basket and replied. Temma's mother, still kneeling in the dirt, tossed a tuber at him. It bounced off his chest and missed the basket. He protested too loudly, and she laughed happily. She tried again and missed again. After several tries, she finally landed the tuber in the basket and went back to digging. He gave her a mock tongue-lashing, which she seemed to return with mock gusto. The next tuber she also pitched at him. This time it bounced off his belly and off the bottom of the basket. He screeched joyously at this show of ineptness, castigating her haughtily. She pitched it again and caught him right in the privates.

The force of the tossed tuber hitting his genitals wasn't hard, and Temma's mother made sympathetic sounds as he winced and staggered back. She put her hand on his hip to steady him and patted the offended area once gently with apologetic words. He flinched a bit at this but seemed none the worse for wear. She placed the tuber in the basket carefully and leaned back on her haunches. He stood with the laden basket in his hands, bouncing from one leg to the other in latent discomfort as they exchanged comforting words. He seemed to be explaining something to her. Her tone turned mischievous again, and she tossed a pinch of dust at his belly. He laughed mockingly and replied in a haughty tone. She pitched more dust at him, this time directly on his privates. Petron felt a thrill in his belly at the tone she was taking. The last of the sun was tinting the tops of the bushes and gave the man a golden crown of light. She was in the shadows still. She was talking, and threw a handful of dirt, again at his pendulous genitals. His tone grew boasting. He hoisted the basket up over his head and arched his back, thrusting his hips forward. His words were great and swelling and proud.

With a sudden move that left Petron breathless, Temma's

mother reached out with both hands and seized the proffered privates in a firm grip, coming up from below and encircling them at the base. Caught, the man gasped and rose up on tiptoes, trapped between his heavy tuberous burden and his captured genitals. She answered him, laughing with each syllable, wringing her hands carefully back and forth for an ever-tighter grip. Petron could feel his own manhood stirring in sympathy. The man replied, breathless. She continued, not laughing now. She was obviously pressing upward with some force, for Petron could see that she was lifting him a bit, but the sounds of his tone were not those of pain. She asked him a question. He did not answer, and so she squeezed harder and asked again, more insistently. He started to reply, but she cut off his answer by leaning forward and engulfing his engorged member in her mouth. He shook and gasped. Petron watched, aghast, frightened and fascinated, as she ingested his member again and again. The man's breath grew ragged and heavier, and then suddenly she released him. He staggered back, the basket still in his hands, his privates bouncing free. She leaped to her feet with a laugh and ran almost directly at Petron, who froze. As she passed him by, unaware, he caught sight of a tracery of fine lines on her naked hips, marking out the pattern of fish scales. The man, left behind, hesitated only a moment, then dropped the basket of tubers and dashed after her, his manhood a hand-span ahead of him.

The frenzied pair crashed off into the bushes, going down in a tangle just out of sight. Peals of laughter rose up, along with gasps of discovery. There was a hurried, breathless conversation, then the sounds of coupling erupted. Petron put his hand on his own staff, and as their voices rose to a crescendo he joined them. In an instant he was done, but their own celebrations continued. Drained but not satiated, he lay there, listening to their ongoing music, his own body still bothered but unable to respond. Not wanting to be discovered himself, he rolled to his feet, turning away from the sounds from the bushes. He stood ... and immediately saw Temma standing not a stride away.

Temma was standing stock still, a blank look on her face, her finger dangling from the corner of her slack mouth. When Petron stood she looked his way, her gaze pausing for a moment on his waving flag, then she looked back towards where her mother went, her expression unchanged. Petron suffered a wave of confusion as embarrassment washed over him. He put a hand over his privates, to cover himself, and headed for the village. He looked back, and she was still standing there, unmoving, staring off into the bushes after her straying mother. Petron went back and picked her up. She let him, wrapping her legs around his waist and slowly putting her arms around his shoulders. He carried her back to the village, arriving just as darkness settled in. He took her to the great house where the other villagers were gathering. He placed her down into his own hammock and sat down beside her. All around the other villagers settled in for the night. Petron watched until she fell asleep, then sat alone for hours more, listening to the sounds of the night.

The next day, Temma seemed little worse for wear after the incident at the tuber field. Petron watched her, to see if she seemed angry or sad or even upset, but she was her usual self. He wondered if she had witnessed such events before. The language lessons continued, as did the fishing. Bighair was ever more distracted by the boats and their coming and going, and the trio was finding fewer and fewer fish. Petron moved their fishing grounds a bit further from the village, and their catch improved. When they broke for the mid-day pause, Petron wandered the village alone. He avoided her parents, unsure of what he or they would do had he confronted one or the other. He wondered if Temma's father knew, or even cared.

Several days after the bug bite incident, Temma hauled Petron back to the village healer during lunch. She explained in a mix of tongues and gestures that the healer wanted to see if Petron was healing well. He had been stiff and weak afterward, especially the third day, but was now feeling better. The healer was again seated in her hut, with the teenage girls peering out of the wall at them. Petron submitted to a thorough exam of poking and prodding, after which the old woman chased them both out of her hut. Petron assumed that meant he would be fine.

"Who are those girls in her hut?" Petron asked Temma as they walked back towards the main body of huts.

"Girls hut?" Temma asked back. Petron repeated the question with hand gestures. Temma watched for a moment, then considered.

"Girls not women," she said. "Girls sick at night alone. Want be good night alone, girls go women now." She nodded to affirm her own tangled statement. Petron considered this for a moment, trying to decide if it was worth deciphering. Before he came to a conclusion, Temma posed a question of her own. "You go night alone boy go man?"

"What?" Petron asked. "Night alone? Boy go man?"

Temma nodded. "Boy go man," she repeated, miming with her hands something small getting larger.

"Boys grow up to be men," Petron said. "Girls grow up to be women." He added his own pantomime, throwing in what he hoped would be gender appropriate gestures. Temma seemed to understand. "Night alone?" He asked next.

"Boy go night alone, boy go man," Temma said. "Girl go night alone, girl go woman. Petron go night alone?"

"Petron already go man," Petron replied, unsure. "Petron not know night alone."

Temma looked puzzled over this. She looked off into the distance, then back at Petron. She pointed at something, possibly the hill. "Petron go night alone there?"

Petron shrugged in confusion. Temma looked at him, at the cluster of huts, at the sun, then beckoned him to follow. With her in the lead, the two headed off into the brush, following the same path they had taken days before up the side of the hill.

As they walked Petron considered the events of the previous night. He was no stranger to sex, but it had unnerved him to get caught by a child while peeping an illicit rendezvous, especially when the child was the daughter of one of the participants. He had been longing for his clothes, feeling particularly naked that day. Temma seemed no different, though.

The hike up went quicker than before, probably because Temma knew where she was going and they were not stopping for sightseeing. They passed the point they had reached before and continued higher. Along the way, Temma chattered as usual. It occurred to Petron for the first time that for all her talking Temma did not seem terribly interested in listening. He remained silent and let her talk. He watched the beach fall away below. It was relatively empty. There were some children beachcombing the rocks and a man and woman a bit further ahead. Petron thought he recognized the children, being a few that slept near him. Petron felt that familiar itch to be out at sea rather than trapped on the island by his poor language skills.

The scrub was thinning out now, and the path getting stonier. Temma was slowing down now, looking around more. She was looking for something.

"What are you looking for?" Petron asked her.

"Look hut rock night alone," she replied.

"Of course," Petron replied sardonically. As she paused to scan a nearby rock field, he looked about, his gaze raking the horizon. He could see the characteristic clouds again, the ones he was sure marked an island. He also could see another cluster of clouds further to lee. Glancing down at the beach he could see that the children were clustered around something of interest in the rocks. The couple was wading through the surf around a rocky outcropping. Looking ahead he could see that there was a sort of plateau up ahead. Temma was moving on, so he followed.

They came to a spot where the path was bordered by a cliff on one side and a field of rock on the other. Temma stopped, looking up the cliff. She started to climb up, but Petron called her back.

"We don't have time for climbing," he said. "It's too steep anyway."

"Hut rock night alone," Temma said, pointing upward. "Boy go man hut rock, maybe."

"We need to get back to fishing," Petron said. "Kita harus memeluk ikan," he said roughly.

Temma snickered and covered her mouth with her hand. "Ikan terlalu dingin untuk memeluk," she replied and laughed. She then turned up-slope and pointed. "That I you here look, maybe, strong," she said, looking back at him. She stood there waiting, and hung her finger negligently from the corner of her mouth like she had back in the tuber field. Petron turned away, suddenly embarrassed. He pointed up to where the path continued up the hill.

"Let's go up," he said and started up. Temma looked back up the cliff, then up the path, then back up the cliff, then shrugged a frustrated shrug and followed.

The plateau was a bit further than it looked, but they made it. Petron was surprised to find a clearing swept in the dust, ringed by placed stones. At the cardinal points, there were small pillars of rock. Outside the circle of stones were larger mounds of stone. At the base of these pillars were placed various objects. Petron could see what looked like palm-sized pads of leather, and head-dresses of feathers, and various clubs and knives and spears. He expected that these were some sort of tribal fetishes so he did not approach them. To his surprise, there was no spirit face anywhere he could see. Temma stayed outside the circle.

Petron wondered about the odd spacing of the pillars. He stood in the center of the ring and looked at each, curious. Then he looked past one and understood immediately. On the horizon past each pillar was a cluster of clouds, the type that marked the location of an island. There were not one or two islands nearby, but dozens. It was obvious that the circle was a map of the archipelago. Petron stood, stunned, looking at each in turn until Temma called him back to reality. He followed her back down the path, his mind awhirl at the opportunities. He now knew for certain that he had to get on a boat. He determined to go back up after supper and figure out which island was closest.

As he walked down the path Petron could see the children on the beach moving back to the village. From such a distance Petron could not tell the gender by the usual reliable method, but by their gait they appeared to be boys. Petron's gaze followed the children to the huts, then retraced their steps looking for the couple. He spotted them just past the rocks, in the shade of a small boulder. It was obvious even from a distance that the couple was hot in the middle of lovemaking, concealed from the village but not from above. Petron felt a stir in his loins. For a moment, Petron thought the woman might be Temma's mother, and he had a flash of both panic and odd desire. He covered himself for a moment until he realized that Temma was too far ahead to notice. The passing shrubbery soon concealed the amorous couple, leaving Petron to ponder his own awkward response.

That evening Petron again went up the hill. Temma stayed behind, but Bighair came along instead. He was good company, although less talkative than Temma. He also paused at the cliff, pointing and talking, tapping himself on the chest. He talked faster than Temma, though, so Petron did not get as much from the conversation. Together they climbed to the plateau. Bighair surprised Petron by immediately starting a sort of ritual, singing out a chant as soon as they reached the circle and going to each of the four cardinal points. At each pillar, he would touch them and sing something to them. What surprised Petron, even more, was how he treated the pillars for the other islands. He threw a stone at a few, he hit one with a stick, he spat on a couple. This done, he motioned to Petron to follow suit. Petron performed a rough imitation of the routine. With the initiation done, Petron could study the scene. One of the pillars that represented the islands indeed seemed closer. Petron pointed out each in turn, allowing Bighair a chance to expound on each. Mostly what Petron got from the expositions was that none of the neighboring islands was as good at fishing. Petron thought he learned the names of each. When there seemed to be nothing more he could learn, Petron led the way out of the circle and home.

As had Temma earlier, Bighair eventually took the lead on the path down. This time the beach was empty, and Petron found himself staring at Bighair as they descended. Petron actually knew little about the boy. He wasn't sure who the lad's parents were. He mentally inventoried the locals, trying to make a match.

If he tried to pick out a parent for the boy based on the adult's behavior, none of the adults matched. There were plenty of local women who could be the mother; it seemed that most all the adult females were either pregnant, nursing, or chasing around a toddler, so there were plenty of women who were the right age.

The list of men who could be Bighair's father was shorter. Petron ran through it a few times in his head. There didn't seem to be as many men in the village as there were women. There didn't even seem to be as many men as there were pregnant women. Petron wondered at that. Could they be on a journey to one of the other islands? Petron considered the boats he had seen so far. While they were large, none were as large as the ship that had brought him to the tropics. By his standards, none seemed terribly seaworthy. From his travels, he knew the folk on these islands usually had larger craft. It made sense that these larger boats were away, possibly on a trading expedition. Petron could feel excitement building inside himself at the idea of a larger boat returning and taking him off the island, for surely one of the other islands had a deep port and a connection to the outside world.

Petron let Bighair run ahead to the village. The sun was lowering but not yet down, so Petron sought the solitude of the empty beach he had seen from above. He walked down to the rocks where the children had been scavenging, then waded around the rocky outcropping to the free beach beyond. Petron slowly and cautiously moved through the scattered coral boulders until he was sure the previous occupants were truly gone. Petron could still see the disturbed sand where they had tussled. He pushed on, walking until the sand was undisturbed. Taking care to avoid the loose sand, for fear of other black bugs, he sat down on the beach and watched the waves. He let his thoughts wander far, back to the home he had left and the ports he had visited since leaving it.

CHAPTER THREE

The Natives

Petron had been a simple deckhand when he first set sail from home. That ship, the Fairweather, never sailed far out of sight of land, plying the local trade routes. After a while, Petron moved to a larger ship that sailed far out to sea, navigating by the currents and waves. That ship had been chartered for a trading run to the tropics. The voyage took months and ended badly with the ship foundering and the crew in small boats. The last Petron had seen of any of them was in a storm somewhere in the area. Now, sitting on the beach, the warm waves washing over his bare body, Petron stared out into the sunset and wondered where his crewmates were, what welcoming islands they may have found, and what exotic native ladies they might now be consorting with.

Petron had seen many different cultures on the trip south. The skin of the natives of each port grew progressively darker, and the features of those same natives resembled those of his fellow sailors less and less. He had seen Slith again, once or twice, and had actually had a shockingly normal conversation with one. He had lost the ability to understand the local languages after the first few port calls; by the tenth, no one on the boat spoke the local language. Fortunately, there was a rough sailor's tongue in use all along the coasts, and that served well enough. When all else failed, the universal language was the color of silver.

Petron had enjoyed the wide variety of life he had found along the journey. He had sampled the sights and sounds and flavors of each port along the way. Like all sailors, he had sampled the spirits, be they ale or beer or liquor or wine. Once or twice he had also sampled the locals themselves. Petron had not left his home port a virgin, but he was wise enough to know the dangers of love in a port town and avoided the easy company that attached itself to stray sailors. More than once, though, a tender-eyed girl had attached herself to him during an extended leave, hoping perhaps to get a taste of something exotic themselves. Perhaps it was the baker's apprentice or the port master's daughter. A tour of the city and a shared bottle of wine had left the new couple to welcome the sunrise from the same bed. Every time, though, that tender face was absent when it came time to go.

As a youth growing up it had always been assumed that a family life awaited him. Now that assumption seemed less sure, and that bothered him. Petron thought about Temma and Bighair and the other children. They bickered and fussed and needed constant attention, but there was just this satisfaction from the way they seized every moment, every opportunity to learn and to do something new, something more. He knew, somewhere inside himself, that he would not be satisfied with a life alone. But that life lay an ocean away, and he needed to get there. Petron resolved that his time marooned on the island needed to end. It was time to secure a ride home.

His language lessons had been progressing well, he thought. Perhaps the time had come to put them to the test. Temma's father seemed to be the chief here. Petron resolved to go to him tomorrow and ask for a seat on a boat. Maybe it would just be a fishing trip, at first, but it would lead to a ride off the island. Petron was sure that he could handle any role they might ask him to play aboard.

The boats themselves were much simpler than the ships Petron knew. A single hull hacked from a single tree was the majority of the boat. Petron wondered where they had found the tree trunk, for no tree on the island seemed big enough to make such a large dugout. Two outriggers were lashed on with two supports, leaving enough room for the crew to wield paddles over the sides. These tiny ships were the simplest of galleys, but Petron didn't care. He would sail a coracle in a storm if it came to that. He hoped that Temma's father would not make that necessary.

The thought of Temma's father brought back the thought of Temma's mother, and the thought of Temma's mother brought another unexpected twang from below his navel. Petron shook his head. How brazen she had been, dallying in view of her own child! Of course, she may not have known the girl was there -- Petron had not. And, too, given the closeness of the houses here it would be difficult for any romance to consummate without risking some sort of exposure.

Petron thought back to his own first taste of love. It had come when he was just getting his own first growth. A neighbor had been hurt, and the man's sister had sent her daughter to tend him while he recovered. Petron immediately noticed her, and she immediately noticed him. Theirs was less of a romance than an exploration that culminated in a long night of experimentation together. That night repeated itself twice more before the uncle was well and the niece sent home a bit wiser than she arrived. It was years before Petron found that sort of friendship again, and never so intensely.

The sun slipped under the ocean, and Petron picked himself up and dusted himself off. He stretched, wrapping his arms over his head and rising on his toes. He felt the nascent tension from his fond remembrances enliven his body for a moment, then fade as everything relaxed. He turned back to home, admiring the sunset as he walked. As he approached the rocky outcropping he spotted a figure moving in between the boulders. He slowed, a feeling of premonition seizing him. With the sky still glowing, the person was mostly silhouetted, making identification hard. Petron stopped beside a boulder. The person picked their way out through the rocks to where a small bay formed. The long legs and prominent breasts told that this was a woman of the village. She slipped into the waters and swam away from shore.

Petron moved closer to the rocks as she swam away. Words fled from his mind, and those memories he had just put away came back to him. He watched her splash through the surf as he mounted the rocks surrounding the pool. Standing there in the open air, the cloak of darkness slowly concealing him, he allowed his body to fully express what he had been suppressing for longer than he had admitted. As the woman circled back Petron deliberately sat on a partially submerged boulder and waited, his shins dangling in the water, his obvious ardor visible to any who looked.

The woman swam back to the rocks at a surprising clip, approaching the far side of the small inlet. She popped up out of the water, springing immediately to her feet. In the orange light, her nude body glinted with a blue hue as she shook the water from her hair. Petron made no sound, but she turned and looked right at him. Silhouetted against the light, she was not identifiable, but in his heart, Petron was sure this was Temma's mother; he knew it just had to be her. Petron stayed right where he was, unmoving, part of his mind telling him what a bad idea this was and part of his mind forbidding him to leave.

The woman stood unmoving for a moment, looking at Petron. She slowly slicked back her hair. The blue colored her bare flanks in the dying light of day, and Petron wondered if she had painted some new pattern on her body, blue to match the ocean, like a priestess of some oceanic deity. He watched as she slowly wiped her hands down the front of her body from shoulder to thigh, once, and twice, and a third time, slowly and deliberately. The fourth time her right hand stopped at her breasts, and her left at her loins. Petron had to force himself to not hide his own reaction. The expression on the man's face in the tuber field came to his mind, and his heart pounded. He slowly leaned back on his arms, allowing the fading light to play across his body. Seeing his resolve, she stepped forward and dove toward him.

She crossed the pool of water like a bolt from a crossbow. Petron's heart had barely beat thrice before her head emerged from the water right before Petron's splayed knees. His heart caught in his chest as her body emerged out of the water, moving closer, her face in shadow but her eyes wide. She reached out her arms, laying her hands on his open thighs and lifted herself up. Petron knew two things in that instant: her grip was like cold iron, and the blue he saw was not a hint of light or a splash of paint but rather the color of her skin over her entire body. His thighs were pinned under her weight, but he put his feet together, and felt her naked body slip over his shins, his toes coming to rest over her sex. Suddenly none of this felt right, and Petron put his hand out to stop her. For the briefest of moments she paused, then lowered her head towards his awaiting member, her eyes not leaving his. As she did so a last glint of light played across her blue face and, with a jolt, he saw that the pupils of her too-large eyes were not round, but slitted. She opened her mouth to receive his pulsing, hot offering, revealing a white row of sharp, serrated teeth. Like black lightning, a forked tongue flicked out and lashed his member.

With a gasp, Petron found his strength and kicked out, flipping her aside. This was not Temma's mother; this was not woman at all, but a monster. It was not a Slith, with their graceful movements and white plumage. This was a predator. He scrambled backward on his hands and backside, gasping in horror. The creature tumbled into the water, and he came to his feet running. He bounded from rock to rock, dashing through the surf and running until he was past the tree line. He looked back, in terror that he was being followed, but the beast was standing on the rock he had vacated, back at the pool. She stood there, a dark figure against the light sky, looking for all the world like any other woman would. The two stood staring at each other for a long moment, then she turned and dove back into the sea.

Petron ran through the scrub, heedless of the scratches on his body, until he reached the great fire. There he stood, shaking. The old healer was there, with a young woman. They were talking as the healer was drawing a pattern on the other woman's belly, between her navel and her tuft of pubic hair. It was a stylized image of a baby. They looked at him curiously, then went back to their conversation, occasionally glancing up at him. He sat down on a bench, panting. Blood from many scratches was running down his own belly, and his loins and his thighs. He scanned the outer darkness furtively. No one else was moving in that dimness.

For many minutes he sat there, beside himself. The other two finished, and the young woman went to the great house. The old healer walked past Petron, her woven palm shawl rustling faintly. She patted him on his head, then walked off into the dark, towards her hut. He watched her go, then realized he was now alone. He sprang up and ran inside the great house. He was greeted by the small sounds of the villagers, who were nestling down for the night, as usual. He quickly went to his hammock, popping Temma out temporarily while he climbed in. He lay there, listening to his heart. He realized he still had his belt on. He slipped his knife from its place and held it in his hand, ready. He lay there a long time, listening, ready.

The next day life seemed to go on as normal. Petron arose and walked through his routine as always, but the very air itself seemed to have a different feel. He looked at each of the children as if they were somehow going to change color. He watched the adults to see if they were watching him. Everywhere he looked he half expected to see creatures or monsters or the very gods themselves, but everyone acted just the way they always did. He caught a glimpse of Temma's mother from a distance, at the great fire, and she looked absolutely normal. The whole morning had a surreal air to it, even though nothing unusual happened. One effect the evening had, though, was to thwart Petron's intent to approach Temma's father about a seat on the boat. Every time he considered approaching the man the image of Temma's mother came to mind, and Petron deferred.

That evening there was a large gathering at the village. Petron could see the preparations underway and slipped away up the hill. The party took the place of dinner, but Petron was able to snatch a bit of dried fish before heading up. He scaled the hill and settled into the plaza on the hill. Sounds from below drifted up, the thud of drums interspersed with the ululation of singing. Petron would occasionally wander over to the path and glance down, but mostly he studied the other islands.

At first, Petron stared off into the distance, trying to see what he could of the islands themselves. As before, the distance limited what he could see. Petron started with the island that corresponded with the pillar that was closest to the plaza. He was able, with a good hard stare, to make out the color of trees and the lighter blue of shallow reefs. Once he felt that he had seen as much of that island as his eyes and the afternoon light would permit, he moved on. Petron rotated rapidly around the plaza, trying to determine which of the other islands he could see best. To his pleasant surprise, forty-five degrees leeward there was another island and he could see tiny dots of what had to be boats.

He immediately scaled a tall rock to get a better view, taking just a moment to check on the progress of the party down below. Satisfied that nothing of note was happening down there, he stared off at the horizon. The objects were impossibly small, but Petron was patient. He could see the barest hint of white and knew it had to be sails. The progress of the boats was painfully slow, but Petron could actually see them moving across the water. Another island lay in that direction, and it appeared that the boats were headed that way. Petron watched their slow progress, wondering what sorts of commerce they were seeking. After a while, it began to seem that the boats were actually moving away, for they were harder and harder to track. Eventually, Petron lost sight of them altogether.

By this time the sun was low in the sky. Much of the hilltop was in shadow. Petron again looked down at the village, then took a cursory look at the island pillars themselves. It was quickly obvious that there were some differences between the islands, at least from a perspective of the artifacts he saw. One pillar was adorned with the empty shells of some large nut, along with what looked like large, broken arrows. Petron had not seen anything like bows or arrows for many months; they did not seem popular this far south. The next pillar had spears and fragments of vests made from some sort of woven beads made from seashells. One was festooned with empty crab shells and stones tied together with twine. Yet another had wooden clubs edged with shark teeth. All had the leathery objects around their bases, and most had flat rocks with some sort of scratches on them. The light was too far gone for Petron to see the markings well, and he did not feel comfortable disturbing the pillars or their artifacts for a closer examination. That would have to wait for another day.

A change in the timbre of the sounds from the village caught his ear, and Petron jumped up on the rock and looked down. A large party of villagers was headed up the hill, carrying torches and wearing some sort of outfits. Petron decided he did not want to meet them up on the hill. He had spotted what looked like another path down, leading down the other side of the hill. He quickly found it again and quit the plaza ahead of the party.

The path wound down the hill through the scrub. The sun had already set on that side of the hill, but the sky was still light enough to walk by. The path curved down and then split, one side going toward the beach, and one side staying in the brush. Petron decided to stay in the brush, fearing that if he ventured out onto the beach he would be more visible from the hill. He followed the path down and around until it once again emerged from the shadow of the hill and the tops of the brush still caught the last of the daylight.

Halfway toward the village, Petron began to see ruins again. He knew he was still not quite to the yam field yet, so these had to be a different set of ruins. Indeed, the blocks were larger, and many were still set one atop another. Petron felt he still had time to kill; he wanted to slip into the village after dark and go straight to his hut. That way, the evening would pass and he would emerge from his hut like everyone else. Hopefully, they would have forgotten his absence from the festivities. If not, well, then, he had been out of the village all afternoon, right? What party? Petron took his time in the ruins.

The carvings on the stones were better here, more clear.

Also more clear was the evidence of a fire. The charred stumps of wooden timbers projected from holes drilled into the stone blocks. It occurred to Petron that the construction of these stones and the building they represented was beyond any capability the villagers had demonstrated. Petron frequently saw debris covered with sand in the corners of the foundations. He took a few moments to uncover some of it. He was surprised to find the burnt remnants of a wooden club edged with shark teeth. He had not seen the like in the village, but he had seen one up on the hill. He continued to examine the ruins, curious what else there was to discover.

He came to a place where a wall still partially stood. Carved in relief on the stone were caricatures of people and animals. The male figures had grotesquely exaggerated features: paddle hands, bowed legs, bull balls, gaping mouths. The female figures were all bland copies of a stylized ideal. There were crabs and fish, birds and what looked like the black bug that had bitten him. His leg ached when he saw that. Most prominent of the animals, though, were the fish, and especially the sharks. A stylized symbol for a shark seemed to fill every niche, and a more realistic version graced many of the carved narratives. It occurred to Petron that he had not seen any spirit faces, which seemed a bit unusual.

What caught Petron's eyes especially were carvings that seemed to show creatures that were half animal and half human. Here was a crab with the head of a woman. There was a fish with the legs and genitals of a man. Carved on a line all their own was a parade of beings that had the heads and fins of fish and the torso and legs of men and women. In his mind's eye, Petron was again sitting on the rock beside the pool, staring into the slitted eyes of a creature that had the breasts of a woman, the eyes of a snake, and the teeth of a moray eel. Were there creatures in the sea here that he had never heard of?

The sun was on the horizon now, and Petron needed to head back. The island was a fairly safe place, but his experience the evening before had shaken his faith in the darkness. He slipped out of the ruin onto a trail that passed between the foundations.

He struck what he figured to be a course toward the village. He hadn't gone far when a flash of color caught his eye. Inside one foundation someone had laid some wreaths of feathers. He turned aside to see them. They were many weeks old, and they had unraveled for the most part. There seemed no particular purpose for them. He turned to go, and saw a shriveled arm sticking awkwardly from the sand.

The arm itself was immediately recognizable, despite the weathering and decay. Petron guessed the owner was many years dead. The sand around the arm was disturbed as if someone had dug to uncover the arm. Petron stood still, shock freezing his limbs. He could feel a chill on his arms, despite the eternally warm air, and his testicles curled up and flattened out. As he stood there the outline of the body under the sand became apparent. Most disturbing was what was sticking up from the sand above where the chest must lay. It looked for all the world like a large arrow. It was just like the ones he had seen broken on the pillar on the hill. Petron left that place and hurried on. The light was all but gone when he slipped into the great house. He threaded his way through to his own place, where he found Temma waiting. To his surprise, she was standing, waiting for him, and not already in the hammock.

"Where you?" she said with a hitch in her voice.

"Up," he said simply and laid down. She sat at his side for a minute, then climbed in. After a few moments, Petron could smell tears, and she sniffled. He drew her close, and she snuggled in against his chest. Her breathing steadied and slowed, and then she was asleep.

The next day Petron and Temma started the day alone. Bighair was nowhere to be seen. Petron asked Temma where he was.

"Kotujo is night alone," she said with an odd tone in her voice. "Boy to man now. He go fish with boat men."

Sure enough, a quick glance up the beach showed more activity at the boats than usual. Petron went close enough to see that Bighair, or Kotujo as Temma now seemed to call him, was now part of the boat crew. Having worked with the boy for many days now, Petron disagreed that he was ready for such work; the boy was still quite small and tended to wander mentally. The decision was not his, however, and when the boats pushed out Kotujo was seated in the rear of the largest. Petron felt a surge of envy; why had they allowed the boy to ride the boats but not Petron? Next, he felt shame for not having learned the language better and not having pressed the issue more. He put both out of his mind and watched as the boats set sail.

Throughout the morning, Petron found himself looking out to sea, both with his eyes and his mind. He could see that Temma was also watching the sea. Their catch was small. At the lunch break Petron lay down for a nap, and she joined him. They arose afterward and had better luck, catching several small fish and one larger one. That evening Bighair (Petron couldn't help but think of him that way) was the guest of honor at dinner, and Petron joined in the revelry. The party lasted long into the night. The next day was largely the same, although now Temma was the one more watchful of the sea than Petron.

Petron began to question Temma about the other islands. She was either unable or unwilling to provide much information. At midday, Petron took her out to the ruins he had discovered behind the hill. She listened carefully as he showed her the carvings, and she expounded for him the fact that these were carvings of people, and of half-people / half-animals, a fact that Petron was fairly sure that he was already aware of. After this redundant briefing the two returned to fishing.

That evening Petron took Temma down to the boats and had her review the parts and operations of the boats with him. As the day faded, Petron and Temma went back to the village, and Petron tried to explain to Temma's father that he wanted to go out with the boats the next day. This took a while with both Temma and Petron talking and much serious listening on the part of Temma's father and many of the other villagers who came by to listen in. Petron did not see Temma's mother, but Bighair was there, with a couple Petron took to be his parents. Even the old healer came by. After a while, Temma climbed up into her lap and sat there, a fact that Petron filed away for future reference.

After Petron and Temma finished talking, Temma's father started to talk. He hadn't said more than a few words when the healer spoke up, pointing at Petron and Bighair and gesturing off across the island. She hadn't finished talking when Temma's father responded testily. This set off an argument that Temma's father settled by standing and shouting until many of the villagers, the healer included, walked off in disgust and fear. Finally, Temma's father said a few words to Petron in a dismissive, if not unkind, tone, and shooed the two away.

As they walked away Temma tried to explain to Petron what had transpired.

"Father says you learn words more, and you go fish boat," she said. "Old mother says you go night alone if Bighair and. Father says you old now, night alone boy." Temma sighed. "Old mother says father is hair inside eyes. Father says old mother is old." Temma looked down at the sand, obviously despondent. Petron patted her on the head as the approached the great hut in the growing dark.

"It's all right," Petron said as they went inside. "I will learn."

The next day Petron threw himself into the language lesson even harder, grilling Temma and drilling with her. They spent the midday break wandering the island, talking and practicing. By the time the boats were drawing near Temma was wearying of the effort, and so Petron sent her off to greet the boats and he hiked up the hill. Halfway up he looked back. There seemed to be an unusually large number of villagers clustered around the boats. Bighair probably had a big day, Petron punned to himself. He tried to pick out which of the children clustered around the boats was Temma, but was unable to. Petron idly wondered what the big deal might be, then lost interest. He continued up the hill to the plaza, but decided to skip past it and go to the ruins instead. He headed down the hill, and then when he came to the fork in the path changed his mind again and descended to the beach.

He had not yet walked this stretch of sand, and so that made a nice diversion. As was the case with the remoter stretches of beach, this one was unmarked after the last high tide. The life of a villager was busy enough to keep them off the beaches for the most part, and they seemed to prefer each other's company to solitude. Petron walked until he reached an outcropping of stone that stretched out into the water. Recalling the strange incident on the rocks by the village, Petron approached these rocks with trepidation. Surmounting a tall rock, he surveyed the outcropping and saw no one. He did notice many very regular stone blocks, however. These blocks, each as large as he was and much heavier, were covered in carvings similar to the ones in the ruins. It dawned on Petron that this must have been some sort of pier once. He wondered how long ago that was. Petron returned to the village at dark to find his hammock empty. He considered going looking for Temma, but decided not to. He fell asleep alone.

Morning found Petron alone. Few people were about, and those that were about seemed very quiet. Temma was nowhere to be seen. Petron got the nets and went fishing. Only one other man was also out fishing, and when the boats launched only one went out. Petron knew something was amiss. He waited and watched. At midday, he took his meager catch to the great fire, where he found Temma. He asked her what was happening, but she just stared at him, her finger in her mouth. He asked again, and she walked off and vanished into the great house.

Petron sat, frustrated and confused by his own lack of understanding, and cleaned his fish. He had finished and was cleaning his knife when Bighair's mother swept past, weeping. She was carrying an armful of flowers. She hustled to the altar where the shark effigies were and dropped the flowers on the altar. She lay there, draped over the altar, and sobbed and wailed. Petron stood there, stunned, as understanding crept into his head. He had not seen Bighair all day. He sheathed his knife and hurried to the great house, scanning the area for any sign of the boy. He found Temma in his hammock.

"Temma, where is Bighair? Where is Kotujo?" She looked up at him, her face smeared with tears. She stared at him blankly for a moment, then her face clenched and she started whimpering. She rolled over, away from him, and he walked away. Outside the house, he stood by the fire-pit, futilely looking for a familiar figure he dreaded never seeing again. Finally, he turned and walked off into the bush, the anguished howls of Kotujo's mother following and haunting him.

CHAPTER FOUR

The Ocean

Petron awoke with a shock, then lay in his hammock for a long moment wondering what had awakened him. The warm island air smelled like smoke, sweat, and sea. Then it struck him ... he was alone. Ever since he had been marooned on the island days and days ago, there had always been at least one of the village children hanging about, day and night. Now he was alone in his hammock in the poor section of the great house. No Temma, no Bighair, no ... Bighair. Petron took a deep, sudden breath. That's right ... Bighair was dead.

For days, nothing had been right in the village, not since the men had returned in the boats with his body. Bighair's death was an oppressive cloy in the air, especially around the great fire. His mother's weeping filled the air at odd hours, and the women of the village spent much of their time comforting her. For two days, only one boat launched, and the fishermen stayed home. Temma was nowhere to be seen. Petron took the net and caught fish, then hiked out to the ruins and explored. He slept alone that first night.

On the second day after Bighair's death, Petron again fished. He found himself weeping at unexpected times, unsure of exactly who he was mourning. There was no food that lunch, and Petron just went back to fishing. There was no food that supper either.

Petron hiked up to the ruins on an empty stomach. He went first, as he had the previous day, to the place where the sharks were carved into the stones. He found himself thinking of this place as the temple, although without a spirit face. He found more stones in the brush nearby, tumbled and buried. On the surfaces that were visible he could see more carvings. These seemed to show battles happening between the animal people and the non-animal people. As he tried to dig around them, he found more broken weapons.

After a while he wandered back to what he thought of as the graveyard. The body was still there, protruding from the sand. Petron just stood there, silent, for a while, emotions churning inside him. A flash of movement broke him from his reverie. It was a small black bug, scurrying along the edge of the wall. Petron thought it was similar to the one that had bitten him, and he tensed. Ever since that episode he was shy around insects. He had wondered how the villagers survived, until Temma pointed out that there were large mats just under the sand around all the huts, to prevent the bugs from biting. Petron had just had the bad luck to be sitting just beyond the mat when he got bit. He wondered now if there were mats in the ruins. He suspected there were, but old ones that were now untrustworthy.

There was still sun left in the sky, and Petron stepped out of the foundation to explore more. He found the ruins of another foundation not far away. It seemed to be older than the other ruins, however. Beyond it was a sort of clearing, where the brush gave way to grasses. Petron wandered through it. All around there were bits of charred wood, many of which seemed to be bits of weapons. In the center of the clearing the grass thinned away, leaving bare sand. In the late afternoon light Petron could see that there were many bits of charcoal about, as well as shark's teeth. A closer look revealed other white bits as well, which Petron finally recognized as human teeth. There were also many small mounds of sand. The red light of the sunset glittered off something metallic in that debris field, and Petron stepped toward it to investigate. He had only taken one step when he saw the foot.

Just like in the graveyard, this foot had been dead a while. There were only a few scraps of dried skin on it. Not far away was a smooth round object that was probably a skull. Petron stopped, looking around. Now that he knew what to look for, he could see that the real graveyard lay all around him. Petron could see the object that was glinting in the sun. It was not metal, but some sort of glass. He stepped closer. It lay on a smooth mound of sand. Petron reached out to touch it, and snatched his hand back when up from the mound erupted a many-legged black creature the size of his hand. Petron leaped backward several steps with a gasp. The creature did not advance, but stayed on the mound, holding several wickedly pointed appendages up threateningly. As if on cue, several more of the bugs also emerged from nearby mounds. Petron turned and ran. He slowed when he reached the trail again, but did not stop until he was home.

On the third day, there was a wake. The women started cooking before dawn, and the men of the village spent the morning combing the shallow waters for certain crustaceans and sea plants. Petron helped the men, his meager command of the language sufficient for the simple task. At noon, the feast began. Bighair's family started a wail that swept across the village. From their hut, they brought out his body, wrapped in fronds and stinking of herbs and putrefaction. The men of the village all took his body, holding it high over their heads and running around the village. They were shouting something about boats, Petron thought, and Bighair, and leaving. Then they started running up the trail toward the hill. Bighair's mother started screaming and chased them. Her husband and family restrained her. The men then carried the body up the hill. After a short while smoke arose into the sky from the top of the hill. The men returned, leaving the pyre to burn itself out. The old healer passed around some sort of intoxicant that smelled like feet and kicked like a crossbow. Temma's father started a chant that the whole village took up, and Petron joined in. The eating started, and the day dissolved into a blur of food and singing and frenzied dancing.

Petron awoke the next day with the sun shining directly in his eyes. This was unusual, because Petron was used to waking up inside the great house. Since the sun was in his eyes, it meant he must be outside, which was an odd thing, and he lay there for a while thinking about this. It was during this time that he realized that he had two heads. He must, since there was no way that one head could possibly feel that large. He tried to sit up, and discovered that he had enough of a headache for two heads. Looking around, Petron saw that he was lying just outside of the door of the great house, which was looking invitingly cool and dark. He crawled inside, lay down, and fell back asleep.

Petron awoke the second time when Temma shook his hammock. She stood there a moment, looking at him, and asked if they were going fishing. Petron said yes. She nodded, and stood there waiting. With a groan, Petron got to his feet. He staggered outside and looked about. It was about the third hour. He saw two people down by the great fire, and one man out fishing. All the boats were still firmly beached. Temma was still at his side, looking at him with a forlorn, almost accusing look. Ignoring both social protocol and prudent custom, he relieved himself against a nearby tree, and headed down to the great fire, Temma in tow. There were at least four people still sleeping around the fire-pit. Petron snagged some leftover food and headed down to the beach, his head pounding with every step. He and Temma began casting, and rather quickly caught a few large fish and a handful of smaller ones. Rather than continuing, Petron took the fish up to the great fire and handed them over to one of the women there. He then returned to the shore with Temma and went back to fishing. After a while Temma's father came down to the beach. He looked like he had a headache as well. He approached Petron directly and asked him a question that sounded all the world to Petron like "Do you want to go out on the boat?" Petron nodded, and Temma's father nodded and walked away.

The boats didn't launch that day. Petron and Temma were joined by a number of the other villagers in gathering food from the shallow waters. That night they ate more sparingly than usual. After supper Petron and Temma walked up into the scrub. Petron led her down to the ruins. He showed her the additional carvings he had found.

"Where is this place?" he asked her, repeating it in his best local. She looked around, and shrugged. She was not talking as much as she had before Bighair died. Petron continued on, exploring in the direction opposite the graveyard, keeping an eye out for the big black bugs. They came to where some trees stood. They were small and bent, like they had been damaged when young and had hardened like that. They bore scars from a fire as well, but they were proper trees, unlike the scrub that covered most the island. Temma looked at the trees curiously while Petron explored. There were interesting stones there -- cylindrical ones. Temma tried climbing the trees while Petron examined the stones. She managed to get herself up into a larger one and sat there, deep in thought.

"Where is Bighair?" she asked after a minute or so of silence.

Petron looked at her, dumbfounded. He had no idea how to respond. He struggled with different ways to say it, and finally opted for the simplest.

"He is gone."

Temma sat and thought. "Gone where?"

More thinking. "I don't know."

Temma sat and thought about this a long time, then began to weep. Petron went to her and reached up his arms. She held out her arms and fell into his, wrapping her legs and arms around him, sobbing. He cried too, their tears mingling and pasting their skin together. After a while his tears subsided, and he held her until she finished weeping. Once she was done crying, he still held her, and began to walk among the ruins.

For days, an idea had been forming in Petron's head. The ruins, the patterns of the fallen stones, the remains of support timbers, the layers of char and the complete lack of old trees almost anywhere all pointed to some large conflagration on the island some years before. He knew of the locals' use of funeral pyres. Given the presence of actual bodies in the sand, he had to conclude that there were too many dead after the great fire, and not enough fuel, so that the dead had to be buried rather than burned, and probably buried in a great pit, for the most part. Somehow, not too long ago, there had been a larger city on the island, and a fire had occurred that wiped out the entire island and most of its inhabitants.

Petron carried Temma until she was too heavy to hold, then lowered her down. She walked, holding his hand. He led her back to the village and down to the great fire. There were villagers there, and Petron found Temma's father seated along on a bench.

"Aku akan pergi dengan anda besok," Petron said in his best approximation of the local accent. Temma's father looked at him for a moment, shrugged, then stood and clapped him on the shoulders.

"Linot meninggalkan dengan air pasang," he responded. Petron understood this to mean, roughly, "We leave with the tide." Petron nodded, and Temma's father smiled again and walked away.

The next day Petron was awake before dawn. He left Temma sleeping in the hammock and wandered down to where the boats were, examining them in the pre-dawn light. After a while Temma joined him. He explained to Temma that he was going with the boats. She seemed upset, but he expected that. She ran off to the village and disappeared into the great hut, something he had not quite expected. He headed down after her to get some food, and found her father there. The big native explained to Petron, with much repetition and hand-waving, that the men would be gathering at the boats in about a hour, and that Petron should be at the boats then. Petron wondered what he would do for the intervening hour, and decided to go fishing. His mind wasn't in it, however, and he mostly just stood and stared at the boats. As soon as one of the men from the village headed for the boats, Petron ran back to the village and stowed his net. A few more men were heading down to the boats, and he joined them. They looked at him as if unsure what to think about his presence, then nodded grimly and continued walking. He fell in behind them.

The boats themselves were quite large and heavy, dugouts carved from some dense and hard wood. The outriggers lent them stability, a feature that their design otherwise did not afford. They were not rigged for sailing, although there were places to mount a mast if desired. Indeed, it appeared that an entire superstructure could be mounted in place of the simple platform they currently had affixed amidships. Petron wondered if the current occupants of the island were the descendants of those people buried at the ruins, or if they had arrived on these boats afterward to find an empty island. He wondered if he would ever find out.

Temma's father arrived and started directing the men to prepare for launch. He paired Petron up with a hale young man named Lasaral. Together they would be set in the center of the boat, just ahead of the platform. The tide was rising, and already the bow of the great canoe was awash. Petron could feel the excitement rising in his gut. He hadn't been on the water in weeks. Wouldn't it be ironic if he somehow managed to get off the island that very day?

The sound of a shrill, blatting voice caught his attention. He turned to see the old healer standing before Temma's father, haranguing him. His heart sank when she pointed at him. He caught a few words like "boy to man" and "night alone" and recalled Temma's statements about when he would be ready for sailing. Temma's father replied with heat, dismissing the old woman. He turned back to the boat, and she grabbed him, squawking angrily. He brushed her off. She pointed at Petron, staring directly at him, and shouted something. Petron could almost understand it. She then turned around and stomped angrily away. Petron looked helplessly at Lasaral, who shrugged and grinned as if to say "women -- who can understand them?", then turned back to work.

It wasn't long before all the other sailors were at the boats. Petron stood at his station in the knee-deep water, watching for a signal. The waves were lifting the bow, and the outrigger was walking across the sand. Temma's father climbed up into the boat, his wet body glistening in the morning sun. The men took this as a signal and began to push the boat out. Petron threw in with them, and soon the dugout was moving. He climbed up in along with the other men, and with them laid into the water with a paddle. They pulled out into the surf and away from the shore.

Petron was no stranger to oars and rowing. He was a bit out of practice, however. He did his best to keep up, but he could see that the other men were compensating for his inability. Fortunately, the boat was soon past the breakers and the work evened out. Petron was able to fall into a rhythm with the other men. This accomplished, his mind was now free to wander a bit. He began to wonder about the other islands.

He had visited many ports of call on his voyage south, and had watched the culture change from temperate, feudal agrarian societies through the more educated, aristocratic commercial societies to the arid nomadic tribal societies and finally to the tropical, isolated, idyllic societies like the village presented. He expected that the other islands would be very similar to this one. The artifacts he had seen represented on the pillars all shared a common level of technology, and he anticipated that the language was probably also very similar.

The boat Petron rode in was itself quite long. Beside it there were two other boats, one at each side. Each had a captain, seated on a platform amidship like Temma's father, who was clearly in charge of this expedition. In one hand, he held a harpoon, and his gaze was fixed intently on the horizon. Petron wasn't able to see much from his seat, but he could see that they had been following some sort of channel though the reefs. The village itself fell behind the curve of the island and out of sight.

Once the channel opened up into deeper waters the men stopped rowing, and lifted two spars. They rigged a sail between the spars and caught the wind. Lasaral indicated that Petron should set down his paddle, although Lasaral himself continued to row, along with a few other men. Petron watched. The smaller crew of oarsmen seemed to be more focused on steering. There were four or so men at the front of the boat that worked the sail, apparently at the command of Temma's father. The rest of the men relaxed.

Petron wondered what sort of technique they used for the actual fishing. He saw no nets or lines. There were plenty of harpoons and crude gaffing hooks. It would seem that they were going to be spearing the fish ... although Petron wasn't quite sure how they would lure the fish close enough.

Petron wondered about the people on the other islands. The island people seemed to live simple lives compared to the lives of the people in the lands just to the north. Those folk were highly religious, with frequent prayers, many temples, and an entire religious class. The villagers on the island had only the shark altar. The people to the north had a caste system, and different castes dressed differently. On the island, except for the old healer, everyone was simply naked save for a belt. The most complicated item of dress he had seen was when Temma made herself a girdle of twine that circled her waist and passed between her legs, disappearing into the cleft in front and re-emerging from the cleft in back. That item of clothing didn't even last the day.

Despite the constant language lessons, Petron hadn't been able to talk to the adults much. In fact, what with his poor command of the language, even most of the children found him boring and wandered off. Temma had explained what she could, but her knowledge was understandably limited. As a result, Petron knew little of the history of the island. He had deduced the part about the fire, but he could still be wrong about that. He did not know if they had been on the island long, or if they were newcomers. He hoped that he would either soon learn more of the tongue, or get off the island.

Petron saw the man ahead of him stiffen, then point. Petron followed his outstretched arm with his gaze, and saw a fleck of white above the waves. Petron's heart thudded in his chest. He couldn't believe his luck! His first trip out, and they see another boat! He quickly quieted his excitement. This was a fishing trip, after all, not a trading expedition; they two boats might not even meet. Still, it was exciting!

To Petron's delight, Temma's father grunted some orders, and the boat turned towards the other sail. Down came the sail and spars. The men that had been relaxing picked up their paddles and lay to it again. Lasaral tapped Petron on the shoulder, and Petron happily took up his paddle and joined in. In moments, all three boats were making excellent headway, their bows sending up spray as they cut into the chop. Petron was struck by the silence the men kept. On the longboats and galleys Petron had been on the oarsmen always had a cadence they chanted to keep time. Usually it was rough and rowdy, unless the galley was chartered, in which case the chant was censored for more delicate ears. In any case, Petron found the silence almost unnerving, and yet the men stayed in step.

Petron ran through a few phrases in his head. He knew the traditional greeting the villagers used: "perdamaian, saudara". Petron was fairly sure from his lessons from Temma that it meant "Hello, brother". He mimed it silently to himself a few times. He replayed in his own head the phrase for "my name is", which sounded like "aku dipanggil". Temma and most of the villagers had trouble with "Petron", and so he had gotten good use from that phrase.

They were closing on the other boat from the rear and to the port. It was a smaller boat, more of a raft than a canoe. Petron could see the sailors on that ship now. They were working some sort of lines off the gunwales, either nets or fishing lines. The sail was down, but the spars -- two like their own boat -- were up. Petron caught glances of them between strokes of the paddle. They were just as brown and naked as he and his fellow crewmen. He took that as a good sign that their language would also be similar. He thought one of those sailors might have been a woman but he was not sure.

A swell blocked Petron's view of the other boat. He put his head down and paddled hard to keep up with the brutal pace the other oarsmen were making. He wondered if they were making such speed on his behalf. It occurred to him that he might not be going back to the island. He felt a sudden pang of regret for not bidding Temma farewell. Perhaps it was just as well -- Petron was not one for long goodbyes. He shook his head to clear it of foolish expectations -- it was unlikely that he would be going with the other boat today.

When Petron looked up he was surprised to see how much progress they had made. They had reached the top of the swell, and the other boat was now in the trough, below them. The other boat was not underway, and they were coming up on it fast. Petron heard one of the sailors from that boat call out, and he saw them look up from their lines. To Petron's surprise, the men of the other boat abandoned their nets, took up their own paddles with a shout and started rowing. It was then that Petron realized that his own boat was not slowing, and that they were on a collision course.

The men on Petron's boat, who until then had worked in silence, suddenly broke out in a shrieking yell. Petron froze, his paddle in mid-air. He looked back at Temma's father, and saw that he also was yelling. Petron looked back forward. The other boat was a scene of chaos, with some sailors standing and pointing and some wielding paddles and one just frozen in fear. Petron looked back at Temma's father again.

"What are you doing!?!" Petron shouted at him, but in an instant he knew what the man was doing. Petron had not signed up for a fishing trip -- he had enlisted in a war party. Petron looked forward just in time to see the other boat almost directly ahead, and almost exactly broadside. He threw down his paddle and seized the side of the great canoe tight as the two boats slammed together.

Petron was thrown forward into the man ahead of him, and Lasaral was thrown into Petron. All around were shouts and screams. The villager in the seat ahead rolled aside, and Petron fell to the bottom of the canoe. He found himself wedged down between two seats, his arms and legs flailing above him. The man he had landed on straddled Petron, towering above and brandishing a harpoon. He was bellowing out a keening cry, and as Petron watched he threw the harpoon, put his foot on the gunwale and leaped off the boat. Petron watched as harpoons and clubs flew above him, and he realized the danger of his own vulnerable position. He struggled to right himself, watching all the while for any attack. All around the screams and shouts continued. Petron finally got a grip on the gunwale and pulled himself up.

Petron's boat had cut across the other boat almost exactly amidships, and had slid almost halfway across. The two hulls formed a rough cross now. The sides of the other ship, which seemed to be woven of some sort of reeds, had shattered, and that boat had tipped. Its outrigger had lifted the rear of Petron's boat, and the other vessel was listing and taking water. The village crew were almost all on the other boat now. Men and bodies were floating in the water and draped across the broken hull of the other ship. The other two boats from the island had pulled up alongside and their crews were busy throwing harpoons at the hapless wights of the stricken boat.

As Petron watched, horror-stricken, one of the bodies draped over the side of the other boat stirred and arose not two arm-lengths away. The man was not dead, but merely wounded, a gash on his head. He looked about at his own boat, broken and invaded. He lifted a heavy wooden club edged with shark teeth, just like the ones Petron had seen in the ruins. Petron could see indecision on the man's desperate face, and could imagine the calculus running through his head; his boat was overrun by invaders and taking on water, all around were enemy craft, and they were far from land. The wounded man made a quick survey of Petron's boat. Petron realized how empty his own boat now was, and reached the same conclusion the other man did at the same moment he did.

The wounded man leaped up on the side of his tipping boat, his eyes on Petron. Petron didn't even have time to look, just seizing a paddle he knew was nearby. Petron raised the paddle just in time to block the blow from the man's war-club. The shark's teeth embedded themselves in the shaft of the oar, and the man landed one foot on the side of Petron's boat. He stood there, straddling the two ships, heaving and wrenching at the club in an effort to free it. Petron clung to the oar, trying to keep it from being wrenched from his grasp. The man shouted at Petron in an almost recognizable tongue. His weight pressing down on both boats was forcing them apart. The waves rolled the two craft a bit, and the wounded man lost his footing and fell into the water. He kept his grip on the club, though.

When Petron felt the man fall, his first instinct was to push the man away, but the paddle twisted in his hands and one end slipped down inside the canoe and wedged there. At that same moment, the club broke free. The wounded man caught the side of the canoe with one hand as he fell, and now he was suspended half in, half out of the water at the canoe's side with the club free. He swung it. It was an awkward swing that Petron was able to block by simply catching the club. He caught it at the edge, however, and felt the bite of the shark's teeth as they embedded themselves in his palm. Then it was Petron's turn to scream.

The two struggled over the club. Petron's injured hand convulsed and failed, and he caught the club with his other hand when the fisherman tried to raise it up for another blow. All the while, the man was still shouting what Petron felt were probably obscenities at him. Petron could not wrench the club away from the other man, and the other man could not overcome Petron enough to climb on-board. They both were trapped. Petron stared down at the wounded man, wanting to shout back that the whole fight was as much a surprise to Petron as to the fishermen, and that he wasn't really their enemy, and that his involvement was just one big mistake. Then a wall of gray arose from the ocean depths below them both. A crack in that wall opened revealing red jaws studded with massive teeth. A dead black eye blinked white, and the jaws closed around the wounded man's waist. His mouth popped open, and his eyes bulged in shock for a moment before the shark pulled him under effortlessly, leaving just a swirl of black water.

Petron bolted upright and scrambled away down the length of the canoe. His breath came in sobs, his heart pounding. He looked around wildly. The fight was dying out along with the crew of the fishing boat. The villagers had been ruthlessly efficient, killing with practiced ease. They were now ransacking the other boat of its gear and catch, shoving the dead overboard when they got in the way. More than once Petron saw the villagers hacking at the dead with knives, taking grisly trophies. Further away the other two boats were busy finishing off the survivors in the water with clubs and harpoons. Grey fins cut through the water here and there. No word of this attack would get back to warn the next fishing crew of the pirates.

Pirates. There could be no other word for it. Petron sat in the canoe, hunched over and watching as the villagers transferred their booty back to their own boat. Having brought no fishing gear or bait, they would now be going home with food and goods just as they had so many times before. Pirates! Every sailor frowned and clenched a fist at that word, whatever tongue it was spoken in, and now Petron found himself living with them.

Once the target boat was emptied of its wealth, there remained the matter of disentangling the two. Two villagers hacked and chopped at the bindings that held the reeds together to form the other vessel until it started to just come apart. Once the attacked boat lost enough integrity they scrambled back to the safety of their own ship. One of them came forward and shooed Petron from his seat. Petron went back to where Lasaral sat, but could not look at him. Within a minute or two the other boat was low enough in the water that the pirates could row free of the wreckage and head for home.

There was no ceremony when they returned. It was just like any other day, with the boats returning with their catch of fish and the women of the village coming out to greet them. Petron wondered if the women knew how their menfolk got their catch, or if they even cared. Among the faces waiting was Temma. She was smiling and hopping up and down with joy to see him. When he climbed out she hugged him and chattered about how happy she was to see him. His stomach churned and he had to resist the urge to push her away. By this time his hand was swollen, and

Temma took him to see the old healer. She rolled her eyes when she saw the wound and took him to her hut. She plunged his hand into a heady-smelling pot of cold liquid that immediately made the hand numb. After a few minutes of that she bandaged the hand and sent him away.

Supper held no allure for him. He kissed Temma and told her to go eat, that he wanted to be alone. She nodded and ran off. He struck off for the bush. He wandered the familiar paths, numb in his heart and head. He had seen dismemberment and death before, with men swept overboard during storms and with limbs being crushed in the tackle or sheets. He had seen fights aboard and in port, and had even had a few altercations himself. None of that mattered. He felt sick to his soul. After a time of wandering he found himself at the graveyard. Looking at the body with the spear in its chest, it all made sense. Pillage and plunder, raid and counter-raid, retaliation and revenge: the people who built the city had been slaughtered, their bodies heaped into a pile and the whole island burned to the ground. It didn't matter if it was Temma's grandparents that had been slaughtered, or who were doing the slaughtering; the violence had lived on.

Petron was at a loss for what to do. His entire hope had been pinned on getting to one of the other islands, in the expectation of eventually catching a ride to the mainland. Now it was evident that the villagers would have no interest in taking him anywhere. Even if Petron could get to another island, he was likely to be killed as a pirate. His heart sank. He eventually just sat on a stone and wept. He stayed there until his tears dried, then continued wandering. He hiked back up the hill to the plaza. Atop the hill, he found the remains of Bighair's funeral pyre, on the other side of the path from the plaza. Petron wondered how Bighair had died. He shook with fury at the villagers for allowing a boy to go sailing out to battle. He could imagine many ways the boy could have met his fate. Petron then recalled the look on the wounded man's face as the shark grabbed him, and he huddled down and wept again. Getting up, he wandered tear-streaked into the plaza. Staring at the pillar with the shark-toothed club he realized what the leathery patches were. Lying there with the old, blackened tokens were now some fresh items, recently harvested from the slaughtered fishermen: hands and genitals and ears and scalps laid out in the sun to dry. Petron stared at them for a few moments, then found himself seasoning them with his own vomit.

It was dark when Petron returned to the great hut. Temma was already there. She awoke and reached out to him. He stared at her for a long moment before laying himself down beside her and allowing her to wrap herself in his arms. He listened to her breathing slow as she fell back asleep. He knew that there was no way she was complicit in the crimes of her fathers, but her still felt tainted by her touch, and he felt dirty for feeling that way. It was a long time before he could sleep.

Petron awoke the next day to the sound of his own name being shouted. He opened his eyes and saw that the sun was just warming the sky. Temma was still at his side. He lay there, still, listening for his name again. He wondered if he had imagined it. Then footsteps approached. Temma's father appeared at the side of his hammock, rage in his eyes and a club in his hand. With an angry yell, he reached down and grabbed Petron by his foot and dragged him out of his hammock and then out of the great hut.

Petron was so surprised by the drop to the ground that at first he did not even resist. Then his indignation arose and he kicked and twisted and clawed at the hand gripping his foot. To his surprise and embarrassment, it did no good. He was help-less to avoid being hauled out onto the beach before the startled villagers. Temma's father was shouting at him, and when Petron tried to rise he swiped at Petron with the club. Petron deflected the blow with his injured hand and was rewarded with a whole world of pain. Temma's father stomped around in front of the vil-lagers, shouting and pointing at Petron, seemingly accusing him of things he couldn't understand. The old healer confronted the man as Petron tried to get up, but Temma's father lunged at Petron, knocking him to the ground again. The healer intervened again, and the two villagers argued. Temma's father strode off to the shark altar and grabbed some colored fabrics. He returned with them and threw them at Petron. It was a long moment before he realized that they were his old clothes. Petron looked at them, shocked, as curses and accusations rained down on him. Where had they been? How had Temma's father gotten them? Why had they not been returned to him? The tirade stopped. Petron looked up. The circle of villagers parted, and there stood Temma's mother. She slowly took in the whole scene, then turned to Temma's father.

"What are you doing?" she asked in the local tongue. Petron could understand her words quite well. It occurred to him that Temma resembled her mother more than her father in many ways. Her father stood now and glared at her mother. He pointed at Petron and the clothes and asked something in a deadly tone. Petron didn't need to parse the grammar to know that he was asking her how she had come to possess Petron's clothes. Temma's mother did not answer. She just turned and stared walking away. Temma's father followed, continuing his questions in that same angry tone. She finally turned on him. Petron could not understand every word she said, but he understood enough, and the woman's posture, tone, and expression were as clear as a ship's bell. It was obvious that, in her eyes, Temma's father was lacking in many categories. She continued her stroll up the beach, Temma's father two steps behind. The whole village followed, with Petron in the rear cradling his outraged hand.

Petron was fortunate that the natives tended toward the expressive side when aroused, since his own command of the language was still tentative. The wild gestures and expressions from Temma's mother made it easier to parse the words she was now spitting at her cuckolded mate. She admitted freely that she was not faithful to him. Petron could gather that from her words, and her expressions, and the parts of her own body she was touching. She seemed to feel no need to deny it, or even to own up to a responsibility for it. He was outraged, but she was dismissive of his demand of faithfulness. It was obvious she felt that he was not the lord of her. Their angry tones carried over the beach. The old healer, having heard enough or fearing worse, picked up Temma and carried the protesting girl back to her own hut. Temma's mother continued her stroll up the beach until she came to the rocks, then waded down into the water. Temma's father waded in after her, his tone shifting from accusation to ultimatum. She responded with a haughty look, and turned away, towards the sea. With a growl, he stepped towards her, club raised.

Temma's mother threw one backwards look at her husband and reached down and touched the fine pattern of scales on her flanks. She said something in a tongue and accent that Petron had never heard. She dropped down, plunging herself under the water. When she stood back up again, Temma's mother was gone. In her place was the blue nightmare from the ocean pool, her skin now covered in scales, her fingers tipped with black talons. The whole village gasped. Temma's father stepped back, his arm lowering the club. Then he raised it again and swung it. Effortlessly the creature swatted the club away with one hand, and seized the man with the other, grappling his arm and tossing him into the water. The villagers all stood, frozen in shock and fear. When the creature spoke, it was a harsh, hissing sound that barely carried any human meaning. Nonetheless, even Petron could understand the gist of what she said. She was leaving them, and she was leaving him. She turned her scaled flank, her wet black hair flipping a spray of drops across the sand. With the grace of a fish she dove into the water, vanishing and re-emerging many body lengths away. The blue face stared back dispassionately for a moment, then vanished again under the waves.

The whole village stood there, silent. Temma's father stood up, standing in the shallows, motionless. Then, his face a mask, he said something in a stern, detached voice. It was simple, and Petron felt he understood it. Temma's mother was dead. There was nothing anyone could do. Everyone should just go back to their lives. After a few moments, the villagers turned and walked away. Petron walked away with the villagers. He kept glancing back, for

fear of pursuit, but Temma's father just stood at the rocks, alone,
staring out to sea.

CHAPTER FIVE

The Sky Above

Petron's feet slapped on the sand in a rough multiple of the waves that washed the beach. The thin bundle on his bare shoulder bounced in time, and the water that erased his footprints splashed over his equally bare loins. He thought he could hear the sounds of the village behind him still, but he did not look back. There was no reason for anyone to be following him as he had not told anyone that after living with the natives for weeks he was leaving the village for a life alone, a stranded sailor far from home. His only two friends did not need him. Bighair, the boy who had been one of his helpers, was dead, presumably killed in a raid on a fishing boat. Temma, the girl who was his other minder, was now in mourning, supposing that her mother, like her friend Bighair, was dead. Petron, like most of the villagers, knew this was not true, but how do you tell a little girl that her mother had abandoned her to become a blue-skinned, scaled monster who lived in the ocean? No, she was now better off with her family.

The last few weeks had been almost like a strange dream. Petron had been bored almost to despair, had almost been seduced by a strange sea-spirit with the body of a woman and the teeth of a shark, had fought in a battle he had no idea he was joining, and had been accused of an affair with the wife of the village elder.

The fact that Temma's mother had been involved in two of those events just made it all the weirder.

It was after the event with Temma's mother that Petron finally decided he could no longer stay in the village. He simply could not be a part of their pirate raids, nor did he want to benefit from them. He certainly did not want to face Temma's father and his club again. That afternoon he gathered up his long-lost clothes and the one net he had made himself and headed out. He felt a pang of guilt over abandoning Temma so soon after the loss of her mother. He stopped by the healer's hut to see the girl. From inside the hut Petron could hear Temma's voice, wailing that her mother was gone, was dead. When he tried to enter, the old healer appeared at the door and shooed him away. She was joined by several of the other village women, who apparently were inside consoling Temma. They pushed Petron away, nattering angrily at him. Saddened but resolute, Petron walked away up the beach.

The island itself was not terribly large. Petron knew that if the villagers wanted to find him they eventually would. He counted on them not wanting to find him. He walked up the beach to where the trail came down the far side of the hill, and then he headed up into the scrub. He hiked in to where the ruins were, and then cut in off the trail. He walked in to where the old carvings were, and climbed up on the wall. From that vantage point, Petron saw what he had come to suspect. The ruins stretched further into the scrub, almost to the water's edge. The shore on that side of the island was rocky, with many outcroppings, and would be difficult to walk. The islanders apparently avoided this side, either for fear of the ruins or because of sheer inconvenience.

Petron spent the last of the morning wandering down through the ruins to the shore. He saw several the black bugs, along with the detritus of war and the remains of the city and its inhabitants. Along the way, he appropriated a series of sticks, spears, and clubs, upgrading whenever a better one came along. Whenever he came to a foundation he would take the stick or spear or whatever and dig near the doorway. More than once he found the remains of a mat buried there. Eventually the scrub gave way to beach again, this time between two rocky outcroppings. Petron hiked back up along the one outcropping, and over to the next little inlet. He progressed this way along the beach until he found a spot where there was a small seep of fresh water from the island down into the sea.

Once he found a source of fresh water, Petron again started investigating the foundations. Climbing the taller ones, he could see that he was approximately two hundred yards downhill from the yam fields. Scraping around the doorways of the local foundations Petron found enough matting to cover the floor of a smaller foundation. He built a small fire-pit where he felt he could conceal a small fire, and he wove a small lean-to as best he could. He took his net and fished in the shallows. He got nothing in the shallow inlet below his new home, but the next inlet over was filled with coral and not sand, and there Petron had better luck. He took his catch and ate, and spread some in the sun to dry, as he had seen the women in the village do. Spying his new-found clothes next to the fire, he suddenly felt his own nakedness as he had not felt it for many days. He decided that if he was not going to live among the villagers then there was no reason to dress like them. He shook out his trousers and pulled them on, stuffing his stray members down into the stiff fabric and tying the drawstring. The blouse he also donned, noting several tears. He sat down next to the drying fish, shooing the flies away, and as he sat he started to weave together bundles of shrubbery. After working for several minutes he stood, and took off the blouse and the trousers, and tossed them aside. Free once more, he set to work weaving. By nightfall he had already assembled two more bundles.

Petron was gratified to wake up alive the next day. He immediately set to work fishing. The fish he had dried the day before was gamey and he threw it into the waves as bait. He was easily able to get as much again. Once he ducked back into the undergrowth when he heard voices, but it was the men leaving on the boats for another raid and rounding the island. He watched them go, emotions warring inside his head, and then went back to fishing. Once he had his catch he worked on a fire. He was able to start one, and using it he cooked his catch. He spent the heat of the day weaving more of the bundles of sticks and wondering if Temma was still crying. Thinking of her reminded him of her mother, and his conflicting responses reminded him of the yam field. As the heat of the day was fading, he left his catch under a broken bit of pottery and crept up into the yam field. Keeping an ear and eye out for villagers, he scouted about until he found a yam plant. He dug it up and took the tuber back to his hideout.

That afternoon, after the boats returned, Petron ventured out into the waves with his bundles of sticks. He tested each for buoyancy. He was disappointed to find that of the four he had, only one would float, and poorly at that. He went back to work, sorting out which types of wood would float and which would not. He cooked the tuber and ate it with his smoked fish and then he went back out and fished some more. He fetched water in a small unbroken pot he found, and he cooked the fish using the non-floating wood for fuel. Finally, he slept.

It was late the next morning when he heard the voices. He was out fishing, and when he heard talking from up the hill he walked back up into the scrub and hid. It sounded like some girls. He crept around the outcropping to get closer. It was two teenagers from the village. They were out hunting for snails and chattering happily. He watched them for a while, hoping that they would not cross the outcropping and see his footprints in the sand. As he crouched there in the shadows, listening to their giggling, he wondered if Temma would look like them when she was older. Suddenly, he knew what Temma would look like. She would be long of leg and broad of shoulder, with wide eyes and dusky skin. She would look exactly like her mother. Petron recalled the last time he had seen Temma's mother, and shuddered.

The girls were as industrious as they were gabby, and covered the outcropping with quick efficiency. Petron wondered what he would do if they crossed over the next outcropping and discovered his secret base. Fortunately, there were a lot of snails on the first outcropping, and they eventually left. He went back to his own little cove and erased his footprints as best he could, and hid for a while. As the heat of the day grew, he hiked back up to the yam field. Staying to the edges, he found more yams and brought them back to his hideout. He waited and wove and watched, and that evening he built up his fire and cooked the yams. He vowed to be more careful.

The next day Petron was up early. He knew from his days in the village that the villagers tended to stay close to the village in the morning. He spent that time picking up his few belongings and relocating further into the ruined city. He reasoned, based on the lack of trails worn into the scrub there, that the villagers did not go into the old city, but stayed at the edges. He found a usable foundation not too far from the beach and cleaned it out, keeping an eye out for bugs and interlopers. This foundation was larger, and had higher walls. There were carvings on the walls, but Petron was too busy to investigate. It took three trips to get all the matting transferred over. Petron was happy to spot a damp spot in the sand near the beach, as that indicated a spring seep where he could possibly get fresh water.

Once the move was made Petron settled in for a bit. He ate some of his fish and what was left of the yams. He gathered some of the floatable wood and took it back to the foundation. He worked on weaving the bundles until he thought he could hear voices. Climbing the foundation, Petron looked around. He spotted the boats, again making their daily journey to sea. He waited until they were well away before venturing out into the water with his net. He made a quick catch, which he took back to his hideaway. He wrapped the catch in some wet seaweed and placed it in the coals of his fire. While it cooked, he worked on his weaving. On one corner of the foundation grew some weedy bushes that gave Petron some shade from the sun. Once, while he was working, he thought he heard his name being called from a distance. He stopped and listened silently for a while, but did not hear the voice again.

At midday, when the sun was hottest, the locals all lay down for a nap. Petron knew this from his time among them. He chose that time to go up to the yam field and dig. He tried to spread his digging out so as not to arouse suspicion. He knew this was a bit silly; the villagers knew he was on the island, and if they wanted to find him they just had to follow the smell of his fire. Still, he didn't want to remind them of his presence. Afternoon was the reverse of the morning. Petron wove until the boats returned, then fished and cooked. As dusk was settling he took his bundles to the water to test them. This time they all floated just fine. Petron dragged them back to the foundation, pleased. He planned to make a boat or raft from the bundles and sail off the island. With the villagers' boats no longer an option, this was the most likely way off the island and back to the mainland.

The pattern for Petron's day was set, and the next day followed it almost exactly. In the late morning, Petron again heard his name being called. This time it was repeated. Petron did not recognize the voice. It seemed to belong to someone female, but it did not sound like Temma. He listened silently while the voice drew nearer, then faded off into the distance. He considered both going out and revealing himself, and moving to another place even more remote. He rejected the first on the same basis that he had used to justify his self-imposed exile, and he rejected the second on the basis that he was already as far away from the village as he could get. He again waited until midday to head up to the yam field, and he again waited until almost night to test that day's production.

Petron's new routine left him plenty of time to think, and recent events gave him plenty to think about. He found himself flinching at shadows, remembering the big black bugs. His time in the shallows was watchful, always looking out for dark shapes slipping through the waves. He considered what he would do if he encountered a blue-skinned woman in the waves. Thinking about Temma's mother left him either nervous, or aroused, or both. The ever-present silence of the landscape gave him little escape from the recurrent bouts of remembrances.

It was in the early evening that Temma finally found him. Petron was sitting in the foundation, weaving a netting to cover the bundles of wood, when he heard his name called simply and clearly. The voice was instantly recognizable. Suspicious, he took up the mostly-whole war club and crept down to until he could see her. She stood alone on the beach, hers the only footprints in the sand. There were lines painted on her body in black and blue, and she was wearing a string girdle like he had seen her make once. She stood staring up into the scrub, as if she knew very well where he was. Petron walked down to where she was standing and waiting, and was surprised, when she ran forward to embrace him, to find that he was crying too. He held her tiny body close until their sobs stopped.

"Petron," she said, "old mother says Petron must talk her today." She nodded, and then took his hand and pulled him up towards the scrub. Petron stood fast, though, and shook his head.

"Aku tidak bisa pergi," he said. "I cannot go to the village."

"Old mother not village," Temma said, tugging his hand. "In not village. In here."

Petron let Temma lead him forward, around the rock outcropping and to a narrow path that led up from the beach and into the scrub. Petron knew he must have crossed over the path several times already without even noticing it. He chided himself for his carelessness. Temma walked up the path in the fading light and Petron followed her, alert for signs of others. The path came to the place where he had shown Temma the carved mer-people, a place he thought of as a temple of sorts. On one of the blocks sat the old healer, her out-sized hat hiding her face.

"Ada anda," the old woman said.

"She says, 'there you are'," Temma translated.

"Yes, here I am," Petron replied. Temma climbed up on the block and sat beside the old healer. Petron was struck at the resemblance. He realized that they must be related somehow. The old woman was probably Temma's grandmother. "What do you want from me?" he asked.

"Aku tahu mengapa anda telah meninggalkan desa," the old woman replied.

"Old mother know why you go village," Temma said.

"Anda harus mengambil ritus dewasa seperti anak."

"Old mother says you night alone if boy and," Temma said. "Boy to man."

"Sampai anda apakah anda akan pernah meninggalkan pulau."

"Old mother says ..." Temma paused with a sob, covering her face. Petron stepped forward, hand out to Temma, but the old healer covered the child with her own arm first. After a moment, Temma spoke again.

"Do night alone or stay here all day, all days all."

She began to cry, and she hopped down off the block and ran to him, hugging his knees. "Petron stay Temma all, all day all. Petron stay."

Petron stood helplessly, looking first at Temma then at the old healer. The darkness was gathering, and he could not see the old woman's expression. Finally, the old healer eased herself off the stone and came and took Temma up in her arms. Temma buried her face in the woman's breast and wept. The old woman pushed back her big hat and looked up at Petron.

"Besok,"she said, and carried Temma off with her into the scrub. "Tomorrow," Petron understood the word to mean. He walked back to the beach and to his exile home, wondering what the next day would bring.

All the next day Petron was listening for Temma's voice. At evening, he was back up at the temple ruins. On schedule the old healer appeared, with Temma in tow. In one hand, she carried a torch.

"Ikuti Linot," the healer said, and turned away. 'Follow us' was the meaning Petron got, and so he followed. Temma took his hand as he walked, and after a few steps Petron picked her up and carried her. The healer led Petron through the dusk to the main path. Petron looked about nervously, but they had the path to themselves. This was normal -- the villagers rarely left the village after dark. The trio wound their way up the hill, past the plaza, and partway down the other side. Petron was getting ready to stop, to explain that he would not go back to the village, when the old woman stopped.

Petron looked about. It was hard to see, but they appeared to be in the same place where Temma had wanted to scale the hill so many days earlier. The old woman said something, and Temma wriggled free of Petron's arms and dropped to the ground. She stood next to the old healer, two pale blurs in the dark illuminated by the flicker and flare of the torch.

"Di sini adalah di mana anda memulai perjalanan anda ke kehidupan," the old woman said in a sing-songy cadence.

"Here you go big, go man, boy to man, walk away long and," Temma said, although Petron got the feeling that she would rather not have to be part of this transaction.

"Di sini kita melewati obor kehidupan anda," chanted the healer, and extended the torch to Petron.

"Here we go torch, to you giving," said Temma. Petron took the torch, and the healer turned and clambered up the hill. Temma looked confused a moment, then followed her up. Petron hesitated a moment, then followed as well. They climbed up the loose slope a dozen yards, and then Petron was surprised and pleased to find that the slope leveled off at the base of a short cliff wall. An area was paved with flat stones, like up at the plaza. In the light of the torch he watched the healer fade away into the face of the cliff. Startled, Petron stepped forward, and saw that there was an opening in the wall. He held up the torch, and saw the healer waiting for him in a short alcove. She beckoned to him, and he stooped and entered. He found himself in a cave. Temma came in also. The healer walked up to Petron and handed him a flat packet wrapped in a leaf.

"Memberi saya obor," she said, extending her hand. Petron understood that simple phrase, and obligingly handed her the torch. The healer started to walk around the cave, which was roughly tubular and twice as high as Petron was tall. She chanted and swung around the torch as if warding off invisible enemies, and her words seemed to carry that very message. Petron noticed a pile of wood lying down on the cave floor in the dim distance, and he noticed a smaller pile of wood at their feet. The healer returned and touched the torch to the wood, setting it afire.

"Anda harus cenderung api sepanjang malam," she said.

"Ummm," Temma thought for a moment, "fire you must, all night, must good you fire and, all." She nodded to herself, satisfied with the effort.

"What?" Petron said. "Say that again?"

"Petron must fire good, keep, all night," Temma amended. She stood with one leg crossed over the other, her finger in her mouth, not looking at either of the adults.

"I'm supposed to keep the fire going?" Petron asked.

Temma nodded.

"Jika api keluar anda akan mati!"

Temma looked at the old healer, startled. "Mengapa dia akan mati?"

The old woman looked at the girl. "Hanya mengatakan apa yang saya katakan!" she chided Temma, pointing at Petron. Temma stood stiffly and repeated her question. "Itulah hanya bagaimana ini bekerja. Jangan khawatir dan mengatakan apa yang saya katakan," the old woman insisted.

Temma looked around the cave, and stepped closer to the two of them. "Fire keep Petron if Petron die all, night keep fire or Petron die and." She looked around the cave again, then stepped to Petron and hugged his leg.

"So I have to stay here and keep the fire going, right?" Petron said. "Keep the fire or I die." Temma nodded. Petron looked at the old healer who also nodded. "Alright, I'll play along." He bent down and unwrapped Temma from his leg and kissed her, then pushed her gently back to the healer. The healer tapped the packet of leaves she had given to Petron. She pulled it open to reveal a crumbly black substance that smelled very sweet. She mimed eating it. Petron nodded, and then the healer pointed back to the back of the cave. She held up the torch, and pointed at the shrinking fire at Petron's feet. He understood. Dropping the packet beside the fire Petron walked back and got some wood. He carefully nursed the fire back to life, noting that the pile of wood he left behind was not all that large.

"Tinggal dengan api sampai pagi," the healer said.

"Stay at fire go morning," Temma said. Petron nodded, and the two walked off into the dark.

The cave itself was largely unremarkable. Petron could see the walls of the tube clearly in the firelight. The rock was black, and looked as if it had been partially melted. Some of it had even hardened as it dripped off the walls, forming spikes of stone. Here and there crystals glittered. He almost expected to find a spirit face carved into the wall, but there was none. Petron wandered down the tube, past the pile of wood. The floor was covered with hard-packed dirt, but the further back he went the more loose rock there was on the floor, and the narrower the floor itself grew. The light also grew dimmer the further from the fire he went, and Petron was forced to go back and feed the fire as it burned lower.

Petron understood what he was undergoing. As a sailor, he had been subjected to a ceremony aboard the ship when they passed a particular port on their voyage south. It was a way of inducting the new sailors into the rough brotherhood of the sea. That ceremony was much more raucous than this one, and had involved acts both degrading and public. Petron suspected this was what Bighair had gone through before he had gone off on his first "fishing expedition". The thought of the young boy being taken into battle angered Petron, and he went back to the door of the cave and considered walking back to his hideaway and rejecting the ceremony. Then he considered that the healer had come alone. This was quite possibly her idea, not the village's, and there could be some special significance to it.

He walked back to the recently fed fire, and sat down. The dirt floor was cold on his bottom, and his testicles dragged through the dust as they shriveled and drew up into his belly. He saw the pack of leaves the healer had given him, and he opened it. He tasted the paste. It was sweet, and not unpleasant. Although it had an odd aftertaste, it was quite edible. He ate it all, licking it off the leaves, then put the leaves in the fire. Being green, they did not burn, but the smoke they made was sweet also, and lent some warmth to the air. Petron did notice that the air in the cave was cooler than the air outside. He wished he had thought to bring his clothes, although the oversight was understandable given the unexpectedness of the activity. He wrapped his arms around himself and held his legs together and moved closer to the fire.

Looking up at the roof, Petron realized that someone had drawn pictures in the soot. He stared at the images dumbly for a long moment before he realized three things. The first was that people must have used the cave a long time for that much soot to have accumulated on the ceiling. The second was that someone had gone to a great deal of effort to draw pictures higher off the ground than he could reach. The third thing he realized was that some of those drawings were very old, for he could see where stone had somehow grown out of the rock wall and covered over some of the drawings, traces of which were still visible under the thinner portions of mineral. Petron stared until the cold from the dirt reached his belly and his teeth started to chatter. It was then that he realized that the fire had gone out.

He leaped to his feet in alarm. There was no flame left, just coals. Petron cursed himself for woolgathering instead of tending the fire. What would they think of him if he couldn't even do what a seven-year old could? Then he realized that he had no intention of going back to the village, regardless of what happened in the cave or of the villagers' opinion of him. Why should he care about a silly fire? He should go back to his hidey-hole and sleep. Somehow he could not, however. He was too curious about what the old healer was up to. Petron pushed the few remaining stick ends into the fire, and while they flared up he walked back and got more wood.

With the fire again burning Petron began to pace. What was he there for, anyway? What could the old healer have in mind? And why should he care? The islanders were pirates, that scourge of every honest sailor's life. Thieves at best, murderers and slavers on average, they were to be killed on sight and avoided if at all possible. How had he fallen in among them? The answer was obvious, of course. Petron had awakened in their midst, and had only discovered their true nature when he went "fishing" with them. On the island, they behaved as normally as any other of the local tribes had. Had he not gone on the boats he would still be blissfully ignorant of their true nature, fishing with Temma and believing that Bighair had been just another youth claimed by Tallagar for his celestial galley. Or at least until Temma's father had discovered that Temma's mother was making a bed-sheet of Petron's clothes.

Petron shook his head. How had that come about? He had been as naked as a baby when he washed up on shore. How had she come upon his clothes? Perhaps she had found them on the beach while out walking. Or perhaps she had come upon him while out walking, and had decided to sample the goods while no one was looking. Petron shook his head silently. He had enough sense about women to know how unlikely it was that a woman would undress a strange man while he was unconscious, no matter how good looking he was. Unless there was a very good reason, Petron considered. Could she have been doing it to help him? Perhaps he had been caught on some rocks, and she had to remove his clothes to free him. That might explain the tears in his blouse. Of course, that did not explain why he had no pants. Perhaps he was foundering in the surf, and she had found it easier to retrieve him naked than clothed. Except that did not explain the tears in his blouse. He tried to visualize her wading out into the waves and hauling him in to shore. When he did that, however, the image that kept coming to mind was of her blue face and sharp teeth hovering above his vulnerable manhood. He shuddered, and not just from the cold.

Another image came to mind. Petron knew now that she could appear as a woman, as well as a monster. Which form had she assumed when she first met him? He could easily envision her gliding up underneath him as he struggled in the waves, swimming effortlessly around his dangling body as he thrashed about trying to save his own life. Had she helped him? Had she watched him, hoping he would drown? Had she perhaps even been responsible for the disaster that had separated him from his ship and his shipmates in the first place?

The fire was again burning low. Petron walked back and gathered up more wood. The pile there was shrinking faster than he expected. Perhaps part of the point of the exercise was to see if the child (or Petron, in this case) was capable of enough maturity and forethought to not burn through the pile of wood before morning. Petron dumped his wood on the fire and stood there a moment watching it. The cold of the cave had all his skin pebbled with goose-flesh. Perhaps the point of the exercise was to see if the applicant was smart enough to step outside the bounds of the test. Petron stepped outside the cave. He could easily gather enough firewood in a few minutes to keep the fire going all night. He considered this idea as he stood outside the cave. The outside air was warmer, and he could feel his body relaxing. He shook his head, and walked back inside. He wasn't sure the exact point of the exercise, but he suspected that gathering wood in the night was not part of it.

Petron carefully rearranged the fire to make the best use of the existing wood, and he walked back to the pile of wood and took inventory. His conviction of a few moments before thinned when he saw how little wood there still was. He walked back up and sat down beside the fire, taking some warmth from it. He still had time to restock if necessary. He leaned back and looked up at the figures drawn on the roof again. He once again marveled at the work required to draw them there.

Petron studied the art on the ceiling. He could make out a series of figures, along with some stylized boats and fish. A suspicion seized him. Sure enough, with only a few moments of looking he could see the sharks in the drawing. He was not surprised to see that there were also drawings of the mer-people as well. Most of them were of fish-headed people with two legs, but at least one looked like a woman with a fish tail. He considered what he could recall of Temma's mother. Her legs had gone blue, he thought, but had remained legs. He wondered what the drawings were supposed to mean.

Petron watched the lights flickering on the roof, making the images appear to move. After a while the light grew dim enough that Petron knew it was again time to get wood. His legs felt especially heavy as he stood. It reminded him of the time when he had gotten stung. He stumped on back and got the wood and fed the fire, then looked up on a hunch as the fire flared back to life. It took a moment for his eyes to find it, but sure enough, there it was, off to one side: a drawing of a big black bug. Petron stared at the drawing. He admired how the artist had so realistically rendered it. The flickering of the flames made it look as if the bug was moving, crawling.

Petron stood there, watching the flickering light of the flaring fire as it made the drawings dance. It wasn't just the bug that seemed to be moving, he could see that now. The other figures were in motion as well. He watched as the figures did a jerky, slow-motion dance in the light of the fire. They seemed to be involved in a battle, with the mer-folk attacking the villagers and the villagers fighting back. He could see one of the larger human figures, a crudely-drawn ithyphallic male, exchanging blows with a shark-headed figure, also male although less well-endowed. Petron stood there and watched the dance over his head. It was as if the whole roof was jittering. He stood there, his eyes roving over the cave ceiling, until he began to shiver. He looked down again to see that the fire was again almost out. His legs were trembling as he walked back and got the wood. He coaxed the fire to life, shaking with cold. He stood and watched the roof again come to life as the wood caught and flared.

This time the story was different. The figures were the same, but the action was much more real. Petron knew what the warning was in the mural. He could see it, drawn right under the dancing black creature. It was waving its envenomed claws over two figures traced in the soot. Petron didn't need any light at all to see that one of those figures was Temma's mother. She had been around back then, for sure; she was probably hundreds, if not thousands, of years old. She looked just the same, with the same long legs, proud breasts and broad shoulders. Right beside that drawing of her was another drawing, also of her, but blue. He could see the scales on her flanks, and the serrated teeth. He trembled at the memory of those teeth terrorizing him at the same time that his member stirred again at the recollection of her manhandling the native boy in the bush. The danger to himself was very real, he could see, foretold from the ages, for drawn right beside her in living color was a picture of himself.

Further away he could see the village men in the boats, slicing through the water, leaving a trail of body parts behind. As their totem, they had mounted Bighair's head on the prow of their ship. Sharks trailed behind them, consuming the dead and the living indiscriminately. Petron felt a wave of anger well up inside him. He seized a burning stick from the fire and hurled it at the sharks on the ceiling.

"Haa!" he cried, venting his fury at the sharks in the drawing. "Haa! Go away! Leave us alone! Haa! Haaaa!"

To his satisfaction, the great gray fish moved away from the boats, milling in a great sea of fins and tails at the perimeter of the light. Petron threw another stick at them and they pulled back even further. He stood and crossed his arms across his chest and watched the drawings milling in confusion. In the drawing of the boat, Temma's father stood and looked at the sharks and shook his crudely-drawn club at Petron. Petron laughed at the impotent gesture. Further afield, the drawing of Temma's mother ran to a nearby wave and dove in, vanishing. Petron knew he would need to keep an eye out for her. The fishing boats, clear of the sharks, dug in with their paddles and escaped. Petron saw a few more coming and tossed twigs at them to warn them. They veered off and vanished.

The fire was burning low again, and Petron was losing his ability to see the sharks on the roof of the cavern. He turned and walked back into the cave to get more wood. The pile was really getting thin, and he decided that he would indeed need to go out and get more wood if he was to last the night. Gathering up the last of the wood in his arms, he headed back to the fire. The motion of his legs as he walked made him aware that he needed to pee, so he took a detour to the side of the cave to relieve himself. He directed the stream across the cave wall, ignoring the drawing of Temma who was waiting impatiently for him to finish so they could go fishing. He shook his head at her, and she shrugged and skipped off with the other children. Petron realized that without the fishing boats to raid the villagers would have a harder time feeding their children, including Temma. He would have to do something about that.

Petron turned to the fire and took a step, and felt something sharp jab into the bottom of his foot. He avoided putting his full weight on that foot by twisting aside suddenly, thus avoiding injury, but at the cost of spilling the bundle of wood and landing on his hip on the hard, cold floor. Petron immediately remembered the big black bugs, and spun about, but he did not see any bugs. Instead he saw many, many sharp projections pointing up from the cave floor. With a jolt, Petron realized that they were shark teeth. Petron slowly stood up, his eyes tracing the rows of teeth lining the cave floor. From what he could see, they were only at the edges of the cave, not in the center where the floor was packed down. Petron looked up at the ceiling, and saw that the dimming fire was allowing the sharks to come back around the villagers' boat. Petron hastily gathered up a few sticks and fed the flames. Again, the sharks drew back. He stood there and watched as the sharks consulted among themselves. He was relieved when they drew back further, until he saw that now there were villagers mixed in with the sharks. Petron watched in fascinated horror as the villagers mated with the sharks; women allowing themselves to be mounted, and men fertilizing the waters with their seed. Eggs were laid, and from these eggs came mer-people. This time it was not one here or one there, but hundreds and thousands of them, spread across the roof like milt in the spawning surf. They were small when hatched, but grew rapidly. They began to creep down the walls of the cave, shark-men and mermaids all working their way off the ceiling. Petron knew what they wanted; they were coming for him.

There was no more wood for the fire, and Petron wasn't sure that the light would stop them anyway. They wanted him out of the way. Up on the roof Temma's mother was standing in the boat with Temma's father, and they were talking and pointing at him. Petron had a sickening feeling in his gut he knew what they were planning. He looked to the north and saw a ship, a rescue ship sent from Braemond. Temma's father pointed at it, and Temma's mother dove into the sea and started swimming toward it. A swarm of mer-people turned and followed her. Petron knew they intended to board her, and subvert the crew, and take her back to Braemond, which would become theirs.

Petron had to warn the ship. He looked around, and saw the drawings of the mer-people almost down to the floor all around. He knew that soon they would be nipping at his feet. He ran for the entrance of the cave, to escape, but it began to close, shark teeth instantly growing from the ceiling and floor. He dove over them, and rolled to his feet. He expected to be outside, but instead he was in another tunnel. He could feel the air coming at him from ahead, though, and he pressed forward. He could not see the cave walls in the dark, but he knew that the mer-people were still there, for he could feel them biting at his feet. He fell to his knees and crawled, avoiding the teeth at the cave edges. He crawled until he was outside, the moon shining palely through the thin, green clouds. He was panting, and cut everywhere. He leaned up against a rock and rested, staring up at the moon. The face in the moon smiled down on him benevolently. He smiled back, relieved that he had escaped the cave. After a brief rest, he would swim out to the ship and warn the crew about the mer-people. Then he could go back to his hut with Temma. He felt tired. He rolled over onto his side and closed his eyes.

The moon does not glow green. On a tropical island, the sand is not icy cold, nor is it hard. And the air is never still and silent. These facts made themselves apparent to Petron as he awoke. He was still in the cave, and he was very cold. His head hurt, as did his feet and hips and shoulders. He rolled painfully to a sitting position, and stared wonderingly up at the walls and roof of the cave. He was not at the mouth of the cave, he knew that. What part of the cave he was in, that he did not know. He had never seen stone glow green before.

Petron's head was pounding. He felt as if he had been drunk for a week. His feet hurt as if he had stubbed every one of his toes, and judging by the pain in his hips and shoulders he knew he had fallen asleep on the hard stone floor of the cave. He did not know the time -- all he knew was pain. He sat and tried to collect his thoughts. The brown paste must have been some sort of drug. He shook his head slowly. That crazy old woman, he thought. Petron stood with difficulty. His arms and legs were stiff with cold, and with the effects of the brown paste. Spots flickered in his vision, and he wobbled. He set his hand on the wall of the cave to steady himself, and drew it back in an instant when he found the wall to be wet and slick. Looking at where his hand had touched he could see a place where the wall glowed a bit brighter, and a bit bluer. He rubbed the wall again, and he could see that the glow was coming from the walls, and that the slime on the walls was green, and was diffusing the glow.

Petron looked around. The cave was essentially a tube, narrower here than at the cave entrance. He expected that it was a straight tube, and that all he had to do was walk in the right direction and he would be back at the cave mouth. He shivered, wishing once again for his clothes, or for any clothing more substantial than the belt that was his only garb. If wishes were fishes, he reminded himself, turned in the direction of the brightest light, and started walking.

The light from the walls was bright enough that he could see to navigate. There was a path worn into the floor, like at the mouth of the cave, but here it was narrower and littered with more debris, as if less used. Overhead there were some icicles of stone hanging down, and the ends of them glowed a dim blue. As he walked, he noticed spots on the walls where the blue light of the walls themselves shown through the green slime growing on them. These seemed to correspond to places where the stone drips from the roof had fallen, possibly clearing the walls of the slime temporarily. Not all the spots were stationary, though. Petron looked closer and saw that there were some worms on the walls that also seemed to glow blue, like fireflies. Petron shook his head in wonder.

The walls of the cave widened, and the light grew brighter. Then the cave ended, in a wall of glowing rubble. Petron slowed to a stop, numb. To his right, he saw a dark blot on the wall about the size of a man. He stared at it for a long moment, trying to let his brain process the fact that he had obviously walked deeper into the cave, not toward the cave mouth. His eyes adjusted to the change of lighting, and he began to recognize the shape affixed to the cave wall. It was a copy of the shark totem that the villagers had made for themselves. It was nestled into a shallow shrine on the wall, and was shaded by dried palm fronds. Instead of the spirit face, there was a crude drawing of one on the ceiling. As Petron studied the shrine more, he saw that what seemed to be debris around the shrine was actually offerings. He saw more of those teeth-studded wooden clubs and spears and harpoons. There were bones, and skulls, human and animal alike. And there were the other things, leathery tokens taken from the victims of the pirate raids. Indeed, Petron could see a set of shriveled genitals hanging from the shark fetish's mouth. They were small, like that of a boy. Petron immediately thought of Bighair, and his eagerness to join the men in their raids. Had he known what it was the men truly were hunting out there?

As Petron stood there staring at the shrine of the shark god, weeks of anger and frustration boiled inside him, roiling his mind and soul. The pain of the night's trial fed into this rage until he burst into an inarticulate howl. Seizing a broken club, he swung at the stuffed shark with a yell. The blade chopped a gash in the preserved skin of the long-dead animal and then bounced off. Petron swung again, and again, chopping chunks of dried skin free. He rained blows down on the shrine too, scattering bones and weapons and mummified body parts across the cave floor. Petron tried to knock the shark down, but blow after blow just shook the carcass. Petron finally threw the club at the head, then seized a post of the shrine itself. Howling incoherently, Petron yanked at the post, eventually wrenching it free. He stepped back, his chest heaving from the sudden exertion, and raised the post over his head like a giant spear. Charging forward with a scream, he thrust the post at the shark's head. The head rolled to one side and the post struck the wall of the cave. The post sank into the loose rubble, and Petron fell forward onto the wall, which collapsed backward, dragging Petron with it.

Petron had expected that the rubble was piled up in front of a solid wall of stone. Indeed, that conclusion was so obvious as to be not even considered. To his surprise, however, he found himself lying on a pile of rocks on the edge of a very large and dimly-illuminated area. He picked himself up and dusted himself off, looking around. He was in a huge cavern filled with an unearthly, dim, blue light. The air was warm, or at least warm compared to the icy cold of the cavern behind him. Petron wrapped his arms around his bare chest and stepped out onto the cavern floor. Turning, Petron looked behind him at the dark tunnel he had just been in. It was as if he had stepped through a door into another world. He could see the fragments of the shattered altar lying amid the bones of the dead in the dark and foreboding shaft. The cavern before him was high and airy, although still very much a cave. Petron studied the high ceiling. It appeared to be made of glowing boulders. Somewhere in the distance water dripped, the sound tiny and high in the huge area. Petron looked at the walls of the cavern, and saw that they also had been decorated with images. Petron stepped toward them, to see what the images had to say, and then he saw it. At first Petron thought it was a low wall made of rubble. Then his eye recognized that there was really only one stone that was close to him. Then he saw that that stone was not surrounded by other stones, or by anything else. Then he saw that the stone was slowly turning, end over end, and drifting gently to the right. The stone was floating in mid-air.

Petron's heart jumped in his chest for fright, and he gasped. He stepped back away from the apparition. Goose-flesh sprang up all across his body, and he could feel the skin on the back of his neck tighten. Every memory and inkling of sense told him that stones don't float in mid-air, and yet right before him was a stone that was floating in mid-air. Petron felt his vision going black, and his knees wobble. The world spun around him.

The impact of his bare bottom on the cold cave floor snapped Petron back to reality. He was still in the blue-lit cave, and it only took a moment for his gaze to find that floating rock again. Indeed, it found two, and then a third, and a fourth and fifth, and then he realized that the air in the cave was filled with floating rocks of every shape and size. Indeed, the boulders that Petron thought were part of the ceiling were actually just floating there. Petron got up slowly and approached the floating stone. He reached out a tentative finger and tapped it. It was hard and very, very light. It spun away from his touch, and he had to move quickly after it to catch it. It felt warm in his hands, and some of the edges felt sharp, like a shattered flint or shard of glass. Petron tossed it up, and it sailed away into the blue dimness. Petron caught another and tossed it up as well, then a third. He noticed that there were rocks lying on the ground that were moving in the drafts of air from his feet. He kicked one, and it broke apart. A quick stab of pain and a line of blood showed where one of the parts cut him. Petron took a hint and decided to look at the wall art.

This art was very similar to the art on the walls of the ruined city above ground. He did notice that some of the images were much larger than the others, and seemed much finer than the others. Those images were set off in their own blocks, and were cut less deep into the cave walls, as if they had been made by an earlier, more talented artist. These larger images seemed to form a sort of narrative, almost like a play in stone. Directly below the carved images were a series of small niches just a few fingers wide and deep. Petron stooped to peer into these. Several were quite empty. A few others had scraps of something lying in them, but Petron could not quite make out what they had been. One, further down the row, had something larger in it. Petron took a quick step back when he recognized the decayed form of one of the black bugs.

From a vantage point a few feet away, Petron examined the tableaux, which centered around a large central figure. He studied the pictures as comprehension blossomed in his brain. The carvings showed men and women gathering the black bugs and bringing them to the cave. The bugs were placed in the niches. After some period of time, the bugs were retrieved. There was some sort of event, and at least one person was eating a bug. Others were holding the bugs disturbingly close to other, more tender areas of their bodies. Then a change began, and after a period of several drawings the people had been replaced with mer-people. Petron shuddered. He continued to scan the carving, casting occasional glances at the niches below. Somehow the bugs were involved in the creation of the mer-people. Petron shook his head. He wanted nothing to do with that, and so turned away. Besides, Petron had an idea, and a new goal. He looked around the cave at all the strange, floating rocks. He had work to do.

In a wasteland, it is surprisingly easy to conceal something, or someone. More than once, as he waited throughout the days on the island, Petron had simply sat quietly and watched as one or more of the villagers just walked right by him. Usually it was one of the village girls, out on a wilderness shopping trip for some sort of food to contribute to the common pot. Once it had been some men, armed with clubs, who were almost certainly looking specifically for him. Once it had been the old healer, sniffing about. Petron had been frightened that she would find him, but she passed him by. And once it had been Temma, walking along morosely and calling his name. That had been hard, because he wanted her to find him.

Usually, however, Petron remained hidden because the villagers really weren't looking for him. Life was busy enough without conducting a manhunt. There was enough food to go around, but it didn't gather itself. The few times the village girls had passed Petron by they were carrying baskets of snails, or seaweed, or some other edible thing. They didn't tend to be in a hurry; one time Petron had to wait while two girls sat on the beach and had an impromptu picnic lunch. Eventually they all went on their way, though, and left him alone again, which was fine. He spent most of the day sleeping, because he spent most of the night working.

The discovery of the floating stone prompted a change of plan for Petron. He had decided to float off the island, not on the ocean, but on the air. He abandoned the wood, and the heavy netting, and began weaving light nets. He would gather the material at dusk, and spend the evening hours weaving. By the time the villagers arose Petron was already asleep. He had abandoned the ruined foundations near the beach in favor of a higher vantage point. Deep in the ruined city there was a natural outcropping of rock. It was barely tall enough to be seen above the trees, and about as long as a house. On the down-slope end stood a monolith. Long ago someone had carved steps into it, and planted a tiny garden on the seaward side, which had worn down to a simple strip of moss. Save for this small patch of vegetation, it was sheer, naked rock, and therefore offered some sanctuary from the crawling vermin of the forest floor. It had a small protected alcove carved into the stone where Petron could sleep, sheltered from the sun and prying eyes.

Petron's plan was simple, and audacious. The rocks floated on air, and so Petron would fill a net with them and fly off the island. Petron knew how to make nets, and there was plenty of material on the island to make nets from. The very night he had discovered the floating rocks he formulated the plan. He had rebuilt the rubble wall and repaired the shattered shrine, then limped home on his cut and bruised feet. He rested that day, gathered food that evening, and as darkness fell started weaving. He didn't know how many rocks he would need to float in the air, but he knew it was only a matter of more net.

The days ran quickly for Petron as he prepared. He did not want to risk detection. He hid his nets in various unvisited places, and was very careful to not expose his position. He knew he would need a simple harness to tie himself to his craft, and he realized after a day or two that he would need some way to make the craft rise and fall in the air on command. So Petron wove, and watched, and waited. As he waited, and wove, he pondered the village, and what he would do once he reached the mainland.

What would he tell them? How would he describe the place he had been living in for so many weeks now?

After days of weaving Petron realize that he need a better gauge of how many stones he would need to lift himself off the ground. He took a small torch and went back to the cave under cover of darkness and dug through the wall. Once in the great chamber he snatched up a floating rock, then paused. He bent down and pressed the rock against the cave floor, then released it. It bobbed back up, higher than his head, then sank back down, almost to his knees, then rose again, oscillating up and down until it reached equilibrium. Petron frowned. That rock could barely lift itself, much less him. He looked up. There were many rocks pressed against the roof of the cave. Perhaps some of them would be better. The problem was how to catch them. He wandered about, studying the cave, until he found a place where the shape of the roof had trapped some floating stone low enough to grab. To his delight, these stones had a definite upward force, requiring some actual effort to hold down. He gathered a few and carried them out. He buried them under a pile of loose stone as he fixed the wall, then carried them out to the open air. Each seemed to carry a faint inner glow, unnoticed in the greater light of the great cavern but obvious in the unlit entry tunnel. Petron didn't even need to relight the torch. To his surprise, the lift each one showed increased as he carried them out. As he rearranged them in his hands to carry his small torch better, one escaped. It shot upward, a dot of faint glow in the night that soon vanished.

Petron waited until he felt he had more than enough net to hold the needed quantity of floating stone, and had a harness and ballast and even a cache of food and water before he ventured again to the cave. He had no desire to be discovered, and the mouth of the cave could easily be seen from the village. Petron slipped in just at dawn with a fresh torch. Working his way to the back of the cave didn't take long, and dismantling the shrine and the wall was quick work. Once inside, however, Petron felt a bit daunted. He could see that it would take many trips to gather enough of the floating stones to make the small craft fly. He gathered up as many of the stones as he could catch and carried them out.

It took twelve days to gather enough of the floating stone to lift the small craft. This gave Petron more time to prepare, and think. Once, on a night when he came to the cave to gather rocks, he discovered fresh, bloody tokens on the shark shrine. The killing had continued in his absence, and Petron vowed to stop it. Petron decided to burn the boats. There was an element of self-preservation in it -- he wanted to prevent the villagers from pursuing him as he escaped. More than that, though, Petron wanted to stop them. He did not know how many men and boys had died in the pirate raids, but he knew it was far too many. There was enough food on and around the island to feed the villagers, so Petron had no fear that the villagers would starve. With no boats the pirates would be forced to hunt and fish and gather for their living. Eventually they would build other boats, but by then perhaps they would have changed for the better.

Petron hid the floating stones in the scrub, tied up in bundles of netting. On the thirteenth day Petron refreshed his stock of food and water and slept, preparing for the evening. He had been studying the winds from the time he had landed on the island, and he knew that they blew seaward from the mainland for most of the day. That was how the island stayed so dry. Only for a hour or so in the morning did they shift, and even then, they did not reverse. Petron would have to take his chances with those winds to ride off the island, and so he slept and waited.

On the morning of the fifteenth day Petron awoke long before dawn. He had gathered all the bundles of floating stone together, and tied them to the harness he had made. One by one he released them to rise and tug at the harness, which he left tied to the ground. The winds still blew offshore, but they were slowing. Now was the time for Petron to make his final farewell to the villagers. He took his old clothes and put them on. Leaving the small craft in the wilderness, he took a lit torch and walked back to the village. He had thought long and hard, and he had decided what to do. As he neared the village he concealed the lit torch with a bit of wet matting. He came to where the boats were pulled up on the beach. Working quickly, he set each boat on fire. Once he was assured they were all quite ablaze he turned and made his escape.

Petron was out of breath by the time he reached his camp, but he did not hesitate. He immediately strapped himself into the harness and checked his supplies and his ballast. The wind had already begun to shift. Petron rechecked all the lines, the held his breath and untied the ground line. He held tight to it as it released, and was both pleased and shocked at how hard it tugged. He was able to hold it in, and waited a moment until he realized there was nothing to wait for any longer. He let go, and watched the ground drop away.

Flying was an art unknown to Petron, and to everyone he had ever met. He expected the wind to carry him, and he had made a large fan to act as a paddle in the air. He had provided plenty of ballast, and had made provision to release the floating stones in small batches, hoping by these two things to be able to rise or descend as needed. Now, as he rose steadily in the night sky, he panicked. He had no idea how high he was! All was dark around, and as the scrub fell away it vanished in the darkness. Fear seized him, and he reached for the release line to jettison the spare rocks, so he could return to earth. It was just then that he heard distant cries. The villagers had discovered the burning boats. Petron froze.

Petron suddenly realized that he could see a light in the direction of the yelling. He was surprised to note that it was not from the direction he had expected. Apparently, the strange craft turned as it flew. Using the fan as a paddle, Petron was able to turn to face the village. The flames of the burning boats appeared from behind a dark shadow, most likely the hilltop. Petron could see figures moving about, no doubt villagers trying to douse the flames. There was no chance they would be able to save the boats -- they had burned for too long. Most likely the bows and sterns would survive, but even if joined they would not make for a very good boat, much less a battle canoe. Petron smiled grimly in the growing dawn.

The floating contraption continued to gain altitude as the sun rose. Petron felt no wind, but the island slowly slipped by beneath his dangling feet. He was glad he thought to dress before flying, because the harness chafed enough even through the canvas pants. He took his fan and stroked the air, but mostly just succeeded in making the harness twist a bit. He stowed the fan and just watched. Soon he saw the sliver of the sunrise, and realized he might very well be the very first person to ever see the sunrise while in the air. For the first time in a long time he felt free.

So quiet was the passage of the floating craft through the air, and so captivating was the scenery around that Petron did not notice when the wind changed direction. It was only when he looked down and realized that the island was getting closer, not farther, that he realized that something was amiss. Further, the new direction the wind had cast him on was not directly back to the island, but was instead taking him at a tangent to the island, and further out to sea. Petron was beside himself, and at a loss as to what to do. He paddled at the air frantically, but again only succeeded in twisting himself around. The wind even picked up, and he was moving even faster. Petron wondered if the air was moving at the same direction lower to the ground, and he released a small stone. That object, once free, leaped away into the morning sky and quickly vanished from sight. Sure enough, the craft sank lower in the air. It did not turn back, however, or slow down.

Petron watched in agitation as the island and the mainland drifted further and further away. The floating craft stopped getting lower, and Petron released another stone, a bigger one. As it floated up and away the craft sank, this time with alarming speed. The descent did not stop until Petron's legs landed in the water. Still the wind tugged Petron seaward. In an effort to get up out of the water Petron released some ballast. The craft lifted and started to climb. The wind picked up, and Petron started to panic. He again released a stone, feeling that it would be better to wait in the water for the wind to shift than to drift helplessly out to sea. As he descended he caught a glimpse of a large, menacing shape moving through the water below, and decided to hold off on the descent. He dumped more ballast. He accidentally dumped too much, and the craft shot skyward. Petron released a few stones, and the craft dropped. Petron went to dump more ballast, to slow the fall, but there was only a handful left. With that overboard the craft was still falling. Petron saw the water rushing up at him and had a vision of himself caught in the twisted wreckage of the craft, trapped and drowning. He unstrapped and dropped free. He hit the water hard but did not hurt himself. He surfaced just in time to catch a last glimpse of the craft as it floated away into the sky. Petron stared after it only a moment, then started swimming toward the distant island.

That evening was a painful one for Petron. He had spent most the day hiding in the shallow water on the backside of the island, listening to the shouts and cries of the villagers as they hunted him. Many times they swept across the scrub, shouting and yelling. The fall and the subsequent swim home had left Petron aching and battered, and the sharp spines of the rocks gave him numerous cuts and scrapes. Fortunately, he had fallen in the water inside the barrier reef, and none of the larger sea creatures had ventured a taste. Not daring to risk coming ashore and being discovered, Petron floated and watched and listened and waited.

The cloak of darkness found Petron weak with hunger and thirst, and badly sunburned. He could barely drag himself off the beach and into the scrub. He took refuge in one of the abandoned foundations. From the far side of the island he could hear the shouting and wailing far into the night. He himself dozed off several times, coming awake with a start each time, fearing discovery. Finally, the shouting died down, and Petron fell asleep for real.

CHAPTER SIX

The Underground

Petron awoke at first light to the sound of someone moving through the brush not far away. Instinctively he lay still as the person first came closer, then moved off. As Petron lay there his memories reassembled themselves; memories of his weeks marooned on this forsaken island populated with incomprehensible naked natives; memories of his flight from the village, driven away by accusations of adultery and by terrifying apparitions of sea-spirits; memories of his work building a strange, airborne device to fly himself off the island; and memories of last night's disastrous attempt to use it. The final set of memories were cemented in place by the lingering acrid odor of smoke that hung in the air, proof that he had not merely dreamed of having torched the villagers' boats, the only reliable way off the island.

Petron soon realized that the hunt for him had resumed. Based on the sound he had heard, the first pass missed him by a dozen paces, but he could not expect that luck to hold for long. Ignoring the many aches and pains that reminded him of the injuries he had sustained during his abortive flight, he abandoned the foundation for a more distant bit of scrub. His earlier days of hiding paid off now, as he had discovered some secret hollows scattered about the scrub. Over the next several hours Petron used them to conceal himself. Despite the repeated sweeps, Petron only had to relocate twice, and eventually the searchers gave up and headed back to the village.

Petron spent the next two days in similar fashion, dodging the men as they hunted him, gathering fruit and tubers to eat and sipping water collected from the seeps. At night, he climbed the spire and slept on the ledge. He left the ledge in the morning, not wanting to risk getting caught there with nowhere to run. The number of searchers seemed to diminish steadily as the time passed. While he hid, Petron had plenty of time to think. He considered and reconsidered his plan, and alternatives. He considered surrender, and suicide, and how those two were almost certainly the same thing. He thought about Temma, and home. He thought about the cave and the floating stones. After a while, he thought hard about the art of the cave walls.

The third day after his fall Petron spent gathering food and supplies and water. The last was the hardest, since he first had to find something to carry it in. Just before morning of the fourth day Petron slipped back into the cave, carrying his goods and brandishing an almost-whole war club. The cave was empty, and Petron quickly lit a fire and made his way to the back. He dug a hole in the wall and moved into the larger cavern, then covered the hole back up as well as he could. Petron set up camp, then hiked around until he found the water that could be heard dripping in the still air. It turned out to be a deep well with steep, wet walls. Far below the lip of the well there was water, into which a seep dripped. An ancient cord attached to an equally old ceramic pitcher. Petron lowered it down and pulled it back full. The water was slightly salty, but potable. Satisfied, Petron returned to the front of the cave, then sat down and started studying the drawings.

It was obvious that whatever magic performed the transformation revolved around the black bugs. They were everywhere in the wall art, appearing large and small, crawling and standing and curled up. It was also obvious that not all efforts at the magical transformation were successful, as skulls were also a persistent theme. Petron studied the postures of the people involved in the magic itself, hoping to see some sort of trigger. He had never been much of one for magic, preferring those methods that could more reliably produce results. Now he was looking to enter into a world that had hitherto been closed to him. The hours passed very slowly, without much to mark them.

Of special interest were the drawings that showed the people holding the bugs. These were all clustered around a central, large carving showing a person with a bug inside their belly. The art around that central image showed various narratives, with different lines of drawing having very similar icons. In one line a person was definitely ingesting a bug whole. The person seemed to morph into some sort of half-fish, half human, and finally ended up a mer-person. A second line of art showed a man with the bug. He was inserting the bug into his rectum. He also morphed into a half-man, half fish creature. The next image in his line showed him as a man again. In both cases, a meal seemed to be involved after the transformation. Petron paused there a long moment, the grotesque nature of the drawings simultaneously repelling and fascinating him. On the wall, the narrative continued. The mer-person was shown eating a fish, and the other narrative showed the man eating fruit from a tree. Petron was not entirely sure what the significance of that was, but tucked it away in his brain for future thought.

Petron examined the niches carefully, including the mummi-fied insect. Each was carved to match the form of the bugs. He suspected he would soon be making a foray back into the daylight, to gather up some of the hated insects. He needed more information, though, about how to trigger the magic, something he wasn't sure was possible for someone as prosaic as himself. All his life he had known that magic was in the world, and more times than he knew he had seen things that could be explained no other way. The fate of Temma's mother was one example, as was, potentially, his own recovery after the bug bite. For all that, though, he himself had never had any inkling of how magic might work. It was wild, unexpected, and frightening.

Petron took it upon himself to examine the wall art, walking around the perimeter of the cave. In most places the floor was clear, having been cleaned long ago of debris. Here and there were places where recent rock falls littered the floor, making progress slow. Fortunately for Petron the air was relatively warm. He had lost the last vestiges of clothing during his escape from the floating machine, and he had not had time to make any other clothes for himself. Happily, it seemed that his nudity would not be a hindrance in the cave any more than it had been anywhere else on the island.

The theme of the black bug continued with the wall art around the cave. A lot of the art of the cave walls showed scenes of daily life - fishing, eating, dancing, weaving. Some showed celebrations, some showed funerals, many of which seemed to be related to the bugs. Some of the scenes drawn were more intimate, with a fair number showing sex in reasonable detail, and one or two showing the inevitable outcome of childbirth. Many scenes showed war. Petron noted that quite a few drawings were worn away, either intentionally or not, and were illegible. There were some carvings mixed in with the drawings, but few were carved with any skill. Petron eventually tired, having made it only half-way around the chamber. He felt weak, and somewhat nauseated. He returned to his camp and ate, then lay down and slept.

Petron awoke some time later, still nauseated but somewhat more rested. He lay still a while, listening. What had awakened him? Had it been a dream? A sound? He listened for a while, but could only hear the ever-present drip. He arose and forced himself to eat and drink. He needed to urinate, but he also was not sure how long he would be hiding in the cave, so he needed to be wise about where he left his own waste. He resumed his walk about the perimeter, noting the wall art he had already seen, and quickly coming back to the place he had left off. He picked up again, looking over the artwork for clues or ideas.

As Petron walked the cave wall he took note of the general layout of the cave. The entrance had been a simple cavern, which in turn connected to a straight tube that narrowed as it went. It terminated in rubble at the shark shrine. Both the entrance chamber and the tunnel had been melted from the stone. This chamber appeared much more like a great hollow. The floating boulders and stones concealed the true ceiling, but Petron expected it was just more stone. The floor had been mostly leveled and packed long ago, but was littered with rockfall. The center of the cavern was filled with the floating rocks, and was mostly impenetrable. Just behind and to the side of this dense clot of aeroliths was the well. Petron had followed the wall and the art half-way around the cave, and was now almost directly opposite his small base camp. The omnipresent blue light had not dimmed, but here the cave wall was broken by another tunnel, which intersected the larger cavern higher up than the entrance did. The rough and crumbling entrance was mostly circular, and a small ramp of non-floating boulders and stones led up into it. Judging by the way the wall art ended neatly at the side of the ramp, Petron assumed that the new tunnel was as old as the cavern.

A thin path picked its way through the jumble of stone and up into the tunnel. The tunnel itself was not glowing, but seemed well-enough lit for a bit of exploring. Indeed, Petron could see where the tunnel ended a few dozen chains in. He started to follow the path. He hadn't gotten far when the nausea, which had never really gone away, reasserted itself. Petron found himself out of breath and his head was pounding. He stopped on a stone to rest, noting how cold it felt. After a few minutes he was able to continue. The path straightened out a bit, but did not branch or widen. The tunnel narrowed, becoming merely as large as a house. Ahead Petron could see crystals glittering in the walls. Only at the very end of the path did it widen, stopping at a small circular clearing. In the center of the clearing were small, round, glowing objects. At first Petron took them for stones, but on closer examination they proved to be mushrooms growing on some sort of dark substrate. Petron was not even a bit surprised to realize it was the decaying carcass of a large shark.

From his vantage point high up in the tunnel Petron could see down to his own tiny camp. It struck him that this place would be much more secure than his original camp in case the villagers decided to break through the wall and look for him in the cavern. Someone had obviously visited not too long ago, for the shark's body was still recognizable as such. He had a better chance of concealment in the stones and boulders than on the cavern floor. He also decided this would be a suitable place for a latrine. Walking back down the path he found a good spot to head into the field of stones, and once concealed he was able to relieve himself without fear of fouling the path. That taken care of, Petron descended to the cavern floor and continued his survey of the wall art.

The tenor of the art continued much as before, with a mix of calm domesticity and violence well seasoned with the ever-present image of the bugs. One scene in particular struck a chord in Petron's mind. It showed a battle of sorts, with one side in boats and one side in buildings. Petron thought he recognized the buildings. It came to him finally; it was the ruins outside on the island. Petron studied the art. There was no easy way to tell from the art which side won. Petron suspected he knew, though. Whether it was this latest batch of pirates or a previous generation, the cultured and landed folk had succumbed to the simple savagery of the sea-folk.

Not much farther along the wall Petron noted an improvement in the quality of the art. Glancing up the line Petron saw that he had just about reached the three-quarters mark of the cavern wall. He also saw that there was a very large and rather detailed carving coming up. Petron tried to step back to see the whole, but the floating stones kept blocking his view. He continued his patient walk along the wall. The art was becoming more grand. In addition to the bugs, sharks were now coming in as a motif. The mer-people, which had played a relatively small part of the wall art so far, started to appear with greater regularity. There was a story going on, for sure, although Petron wasn't entirely sure what. Certain of the figures were drawn or, more frequently, carved, larger. The mer-people seemed to be associated more frequently with the taller characters. Petron reached the big drawing, and stood and studied it. He finally decided it was showing a great battle between two of the figures. One, standing with arms outstretched, looked for all the world like a male version of Temma's mother when she was a mer-person. The other figure, seemingly all human, knelt before the other in defeat. Their weapons seemed to be flames, or rays of light. It was there, above the large carving, that Petron saw the inevitable spirit face. It was large and complex and integrated into the edges of the larger carving.

As Petron stood and studied the spirit face, his eye was drawn to a spot between the large carving and the spirit face. There was something there about the size of his hand, and it seemed to sparkle. It was hard to make it out in the dim blue light, but to Petron's eye it looked like a great red gem. The more he looked at it, in fact, the more sure he was that it was a gem, for he was sure he could see the light shining through it. He looked up and down the wall to see if there were more, but there was only the one. Now he was convinced it was a gem, and he was also convinced that it was glowing. This took him aback, even in an underground room filled with glowing, floating rocks. He stared at it as the glow intensified. Petron shivered nervously and his balls shrunk. In hi smind he thought he could hear voices, indistinct and far away, whispering. He wondered if he should step back away from the wall, in case something happened. He could imagine all the stones falling suddenly. In fact, he could hear something, and turned to see what it was.

Petron froze at what he saw behind him. Where before the cavern had been filled with the floating stones, now all those stones were silently, or mostly silently, rising. What he had heard was the tiny tapping sounds as here and there two would touch. They all rose, and left the entire cavern floor open. There, in the center of the floor, Petron saw something remaining. He studied it, and as recognition dawned in his mind his testicles drew the rest of the way up into his belly and his hair all stood on end. There, in the center of the floor, was a man.

It wasn't a man of flesh and blood; Petron saw that immediately. For one thing, the entire lower half of the person was embedded in some sort of pedestal or stony outcropping. The figure's arms were thrown wide, and the face was tipped back and looking toward the ceiling. Petron edged a bit closer, daring a closer look. The face was contorted in shock and pain, and the muscles stood out in stark relief. With sudden conviction Petron realized this was not a carving -- it was too realistic -- this was the loser himself, turned to stone.

As Petron stood there he noticed that the stones were once again falling slowly downward, and would soon cover over the unhappy soul entombed there. Petron backed away until he was again at the side of the cavern. He watched as the stones quietly covered up the petrified figure. He looked around at the cavern with its wonders, and was overwhelmed by the feeling of being surrounded by magic. Suddenly he felt nauseated again. He quickly walked over to his camp and gathered up his things. He carried them around to the back of the cavern and up to the top. He found a spot off to the side of the mushroom patch and laid it all out. He then lay down, and closed his eyes. As he lay there on the hard dirt, with only the thin woven mat to cushion him, he tried to imagine who the entombed, petrified figure must have been and what he had been fighting for. Images of Temma's mother continued to come to his mind, along with images of sharks, endlessly circling. Finally, he fell asleep.

How long he had been asleep Petron wasn't sure. Why he awoke was also uncertain. The same dim blue light illuminated the rocky alcove where he lay. Petron felt congested, something he had not felt for years. He got up slowly, his body aching and his head swimming. His stomach turned, and he nearly vomited. He stood, eyes closed, for a while before trying to move. It was as he was standing there that he heard the voices.

Whoever was speaking was making no effort to be quiet, and yet their voice was soft. Petron immediately ducked down. He carefully and quietly moved into the nearby stones and hid himself. The voices continued. He listened to them, but was unable to make out what they were saying, both because of the language barrier and because they were muffled. Petron realized that whoever was speaking must still be in the tunnel. He uttered a silent prayer that his awkward repair of the wall escaped detection. He realized that his campsite was still in the open for any to see that might venture up the path, but he decided the noise he would make trying to conceal the camp might give him away, so he just crouched low and stayed quiet. The voices continued for what seemed like an eternity, then faded away slowly enough that Petron didn't realize at first that they were gone. Only when he could no longer stand to crouch did he straighten up, and it was some time before he would venture down to the cavern floor.

Once he was sure he was alone, Petron ate and drank. Afterward he felt stronger and more hopeful. He also knew what he needed. Surrounded by a magical world in the cavern, Petron needed to become part of that world. Somehow, Petron needed to tap into that magic. All his life Petron had heard of magic, and had seen many things that could be explained no other way, but never had anyone ever told him exactly how to make it. He knew the spirit faces were somehow involved, but the details were unknown to him. Now he knew that the red crystal was also involved. Of all the places he had been in his life, if there was magic anywhere, it was in this cave. Somewhere in all that cave art there had to be some mention of where all this magic began. With determination Petron descended on the floor and started walking around the perimeter of the cavern, studying the walls.

After a half a hour or so of study, Petron came across his first hint. Ironically, it was not actually in the art on the wall, but rather in the wall itself. Petron had become slightly more engrossed than he planned in a drawing of what appeared to be several couples engaged in sex when he caught a glimpse of something sparkling off to his right. It turned out to be more of that red crystal. Unlike the great, hand-sized orb over the carved battle scene, this was distributed throughout the matrix of the cave wall itself as many tiny crystals. He had not noticed it before, but once he was stopped he could see the myriad tiny flashes of light. As he stood there, admiring the crystals, he glanced back at the drawings. To his amazement and delight they seemed to be moving. As he watched, the couples rocked back and forth in their amorous play. The more he stood still and watched, more and more of the drawings above and to the sides began to move as well, until it seemed the whole wall was at play. In his mind the whispers were back. Smiling like a little boy, Petron wandered along the wall, enraptured by the scene, until he realized that the art was no longer moving. A quick survey of the stone showed no trace of the red crystals. Petron walked back to the spot where the crystals were and waited, concentrating on the pictures. The effect was more rapid this time, and more pronounced. Petron's heart sang in his chest. He was onto something.

Petron walked rapidly around the cave, looking for more of the red in the rock. In three other places, he found it, and in each case, he could make the pictures dance for him with ease. In one spot, he could actually hear the art singing to him, distinctly above the whispers. He wondered how he was going to translate that into a way off the island. He walked back to the great carving with the large gem, and willed the stone to rise, and fall. It did. Petron tried to move the stone in other ways, however, and it ignored him. It was enchanted, to be sure, but not by him. It was still obeying its original master. Petron sent the stones up and down until his head hurt and his stomach was turning, trying to see if there was anything else, but the stones did not change. After a while he had to pee and headed back up to the rocks. He found his designated area and assumed the position. As he stood and watered the rocks he looked about the great alcove. It was then that he saw the glitter of crystal winking high up at the far end of the tunnel.

Petron finished and almost ran to the top of the path. The highest point of the mushroom patch was only a few armslengths from the wall, and Petron stood and stared up at it. The wall itself was composed of crystals, huge crystals. These were dull, however, and allowed no light through, for the most part. The glinting Petron had seen was the reflection of the light below off smooth surfaces. Disappointment tickled Petron's heart. He stood there anyway, stock still, willing the wall to show him something better. Finally, deep within a large crystal right before him Petron saw the faintest of glimmers. There was magic here, as well. Petron clambered over the debris until he could touch the smooth mineral prism. He could feel its life, and see its glow. Petron embraced the smooth pillar of rock, which was almost as big as he was. He looked up and around, and all over the wall faint glimmers of red answered.

For many minutes Petron balanced precariously atop a short boulder and clung to the crystal, surveying the interior surface of the tunnel, trying to pinpoint the brightest spark he could see. He finally homed in on a particularly vivid crystal not too far away and made his way there. In response to his approach the rock began to glow brighter. Petron got close enough to run his hand over it, and it responded. He studied it, taking in its shape and texture. He controlled his breathing, and was gratified to see the pulse of life inside the rock synchronize itself with his breath. Closing his eyes, Petron tried to visualize the inside of the crystal. He could feel it, inside his head, he was sure of it. Opening his eyes, Petron picked out a stone lying in the mushroom patch not far away. With one hand on the crystal, and with one hand pointed at the stone, Petron mentally commanded to stone to rise. For many long moments, nothing happened, and then nothing continued to happen. Petron finally tired, and went back to examining the crystal.

Petron could see that there was a large crack at the base of the crystal. He wondered if he could somehow break it free from the wall and take it down to some of the other crystals, to see how they could interact. Petron clambered back down to his camp, retrieved the war club, then climbed back up to the crystal. He considered the possible weight of the rock, which was much smaller than the first but formidable nonetheless. Taking care not to leave any part of his body underneath it, Petron wedged the club into the space between the live crystal and a neighbor. He was about to start to pry when there was a loud snap, and the crystal fell free. It hit the rock beside him, and shattered to dust.

Petron's yelp of surprise at the crystal popping free turned into a wail of despair when it disintegrated. This wail in turn became a hacking cough as he accidentally inhaled the very dust his prize turned into. Petron stumbled down off the rocks and onto the smoother floor of the mushroom patch, his chest heaving with cough after cough. He coughed until he was wheezing and his head spun, then finally got to his feet and walked down the path a way, out of the dissipating cloud. It was them that he saw the sparkles, and heard the voices, and felt the breeze. Petron stood, stunned. Where there had been a dimly lit hole in the mountain there was now a realm of light. What had been whispers were now voices, resonant and disctinct. Wisps of mist floated by with elfin faces, singing ethereally. Petron could feel the wind, and smell it too, and he could feel the world spinning. Petron could feel the magic. He willed it, and his body arose, and floated down to the chamber floor.

"You have returned. Welcome."

Petron wondered for a moment where the voice was coming from, and then his new sense of the mystical drew his gaze to the spirit face carved into the wall and he drifted over toward it.

"Returned?" Petron asked, listening to his words being echoed and answered in fragments by the faces and figures that swirled around him. On the wall, the spirit face smiled.

"For many years I have watched the other people come in and out of the cave, but none could wake me, and now here you are. Your people have returned."

"What is this place?"

"The cave of the battle, obviously," came the reply. "Will you now awaken the hero within it?"

"Not now," Perton replied. "First I want to learn how to become a child of the sea."

"Hmmmm," opined the face, "such dangerous magic. Can you not read the warnings carved here?"

"Help me read them," Petron said.

"Very well," the face replied, and more light flooded into Petron's mind.

For what seemed like ages Petron drifted and danced among with the floating stones. He walked all the way around the cavern looking and talking with the wall art. He learned the whole story of the island, of how the original inhabitants grew strong and wise in an isolation that was broken when one member of their race discovered the magic, and began to make followers for himself of the mer-people. Petron watched the war unfold and escalate to the final great battle between the heretic and the hero that gouged out the great cavern and filled it with latent magic. Most importantly, he solidified in his mind what he already suspected; the black bugs were the key to the creation of the mer-people, and only one method -- a terrible, degrading method -- would bring a temporary change.

Just as during his trial in the cave, Petron was not sure of the exact moment the magic wore off. He found himself standing at the lip of the well, staring down inside. All about was silence, broken only by the slow drip of water. He had been replaying his time on the island over and over in his head, lost in a psychedelic funk. Petron pushed himself back away from the edge, suddenly frightened of falling. The rush of blood the fear brought to his head cleared his mind some, and his heartbeat quickened when he realized how much power he had at his disposal: how much power, and how much danger. He had the power now to just fly off the island, if he wanted, but he could not trust that power not to confuse his mind and dump him dazed and lost in the ocean. Perhaps there was another way, however. Petron looked across the cave at where the spirit face was carved. In the dim light he could barely make it out. He walked over to it, and found it again immobile. Petron retained some ability to read the wall art, although not perfectly. Now that he was coming back to himself, the elements of a plan were coming together in his mind. He could become a mer-person for a day, and swim to the mainland. He needed only two things for this, he knew now: magic, and a black bug. Petron knew where both were to be found, and how each was to be employed. All that remained were the ticklish details. Petron set to work.

The easiest and most straightforward part was the magic. He had seen something while in his magic-induced trance. The red crystals held the remnants of the magic unleashed so long ago in the great battle that formed the cavern. Petron had unintentionally released some when he shattered the crystal. If it worked once, he expected it would work again. Petron climbed back up to where the alcove ended. He stood and concentrated until the red glow revealed the presence of the wild magic. Selecting a reasonably sized specimen, Petron again set to prying it free, taking more care to catch it when it fell. Nonetheless, it still cracked in two. Petron could feel reality ripple as the fracturing stone released a bit of its captured glamour.

Sudden inspiration struck him. While the wave of distortion still reverberated in the air, Petron cast his gaze and his focus on the crystals. He wanted red crystals. He could feel the magic in the air. He had wielded this power once before. He willed the magic to himself, and then commanded all the hidden power to reveal itself. In response, the wall lit up as dozens of stone prisms blazed red. Petron focused on the ones easiest to free and carry away, and all but two dimmed. Petron climbed over the debris until he could reach the lowest, and simply lifted it free from the wall. He carefully hauled it down to the mushroom patch, then returned for the other crystal. This one was smaller, but brighter, and higher on the wall. Petron fought his way there, climbing the wall like it was a tree. Once there he was unable to move the crystal, and had to back down and fetch a good-sized rock. He climbed back up, and with a well-aimed tap snapped it off at the base.

With the two crystals safely stowed, Petron settled down for some sleep. He had no idea what time it was outside, or how long it would take to get a bug, so he wanted to be rested. He was able to fall asleep instantly. His dreams were wild and chaotic. In them Temma appeared as a grown woman in sailor's garb and taunted him for having killed her mother. She turned into a shark and spat fire on him which somehow was the coldest thing he had ever felt. He ran away to the keep in Braemond, and spent hours counting the rats as they ran in and out of the sewer grates. When he awoke, he was very stiff and mildly nauseated. He ate some, drank some, peed some, then took the crystals down to where the bug niches were carved in the wall. Returning to the mushroom patch he got the war club, then grabbed the water pitcher from the well. These in hand he walked to the front of the cave. Petron listened intently for many minutes, and heard no movement on the other side of the wall. He broke through, and found the tunnel deserted. He piled the stones back up and crept out the cave.

Even before he reached the mouth of the cave Petron could see the daylight, and could smell the smoke. He stopped at the back of the entrance cavern and waited for his eyes to adjust. When he crept to the mouth of the cave he was stunned by what he saw, and smelled. The air reeked of smoke, and for as far as he could see from the cave all the vegetation was burned away or charred into twisted stumps. The village was still standing, and appeared unharmed, but the scrub was nothing but ash and charcoal as far as he could see. Petron retreated to the dark of the cave to consider. He had one goal and one goal alone; secure a black bug and live to use it. He had planned to move under cover of the scrub, but that hope was now gone. Or was it?

Petron poked his head out of the cave again. The stumps of the trees might provide enough cover for him if he was careful, but he would need to be very vigilant. He might also need to wait until dark. Petron looked up at the sky, and judged the day to be three-quarters gone. Dusk would fall, and then he could move. It might also help if he darkened his skin with some charcoal. Petron set about gathering up the charcoal scattered near where his fire had been, and smearing it on his body. Once darkened, Petron retreated to the back of the cave and waited. He kept the war-club ready, in case he was discovered. Petron plotted out his steps as he sat in the cool darkness. He expected that the best place to find a bug quickly was to go to the great grave pit. It was a considerable distance from the cave, but it gave the greatest chance of success. As he sat it occurred to him that he needed daylight to find the bugs. This prompted him to get up and approach the entrance to the cave. Again, he could see no one, but he could hear shouting. It all seemed to come from the far end of the island. Petron picked out a largish clump of stumps just below where the path was, took one last look around, and made a dash for it.

The run was not a far one, but Petron's heart was hammering in his chest by the time he got there, and his chest was heaving. He pulled up behind the twisted, blackened trunks and stopped, scanning up and down and all about. He was on the lower flank of the island's one large hill, which was now all char and stubble. He could barely make out the village through the thicket, and he could see the top of the hill if he peered around the edge of the trunks. His heart almost stopped when he realized that he could see two men at the top of the hill. He clutched the war club, his mind racing, his imagination trying to think of places to run, places to hide. As he watched them, however, they made no sign that they had seen him. They seemed more focused on the far end of the island. Petron watched them for a long moment, until he was assured they were not coming at him, then he started to plan his moves.

The burial pit was almost exactly on the opposite side of the hill. To reach it Petron would have to circle low enough to stay in the scrub, but still reach the pit before dark. Petron scanned the scrub until he spotted another clump of trunks nearby. He studied the lookouts above, gauged the distance, and then ran for it. He arrived without incident. The lookouts did not move. He repeated the move, with the same result. Petron kept on, moving from spot to spot. Soon he was rounding the hill. To his surprise and relief, he was able to spot what appeared to be unburned foliage towards the far shore. Expecting to be able to make better time there, Petron moved farther and farther away from the hill and closer to the foliage. He had never really considered the unburned scrub to be much of a forest, but compared to the denuded trunks he was hiding in the unburned portion looked lush.

As soon as Petron reached the scrub he dropped all pretense of hiding and moved as fast as possible towards the burial pit. He soon realized that the fires had already reached it, however. To make matters worse, he could now see men posted at intervals along the edge of the unburned wood. There was even one at the far end, not far from where he had entered! He had no idea how he had missed that one, but nonetheless he was now caught behind enemy lines with little time to lose. Petron studied the terrain and plotted a path to the burial site that would provide the best cover. He felt he could make it unseen, and immediately struck out on it. He followed a shallow depression to a narrow alley between two foundations. Sliding up it on his side, he cast glances over the edges of the foundations at the guards, who were quite distant. They seemed intent to watch the forest. The burial site was very exposed, and Petron remembered that it was also alive with nasty creatures. He was on the edge of it now. Even after the fire he could see one of the black devils sunning itself on the central mound. Petron carefully pushed himself out from between the two foundations and onto the sand. He kept moving for fear of getting stung again. He set his eye on a smaller mound not too far away. He had the club ready to dig, and the pitcher ready to hold the creature that he assumed would be just inside the small mound. He was almost upon it when he heard the yell.

Petron immediately snapped his head up. He could see the guard down where he had entered the wood pointing at him and yelling. Petron's heart fell. He looked back at the other guard just as he also saw Petron, and then there were two guards yelling. Petron looked at the central mound, and saw the bug was still there. This was his only chance. He leaped to his feet, sprinted to the center of the burial field and with a single great swipe scooped the entire mound into the pitcher. He then sprinted like a maniac back into the scrub. He plunged as far into it as he could, until he felt he could not be seen, the angled sharply to the side, and ran some more. He ran until he could tell the yells of the far guard were close, and then he stopped stock still. Sure enough, the guard ran right past on the burned side of the woods. As Petron expected, they were hesitant to come into the scrub alone to get him. Once the guard passed Petron continued on, quickly but quietly.

Petron reached the far end of the remaining sliver of scrub and peeked out. What he saw encouraged him. The two men from the hilltop had come down, and were headed at a run towards the burial pit. A hoard of villagers was also coming up from the far end of the island. By now the sun was setting, but Petron could still see clearly enough to know that Temma's father was in the lead. The entire party plunged into the forest, and for a brief, blessed moment there were no prying eyes to see Petron slip out and move away through the remains of the scrub. He was cautious and stuck to cover, and by the time villagers emerged from the scrub to again set up watch Petron was well on his way back to the cave. The return trip was faster, mostly since Petron was less cautious once he rounded the side of the hill. He was fairly certain no one saw him enter the cave, but he expected it would be searched again when they were unable to find him in the remains of the scrub, which they were sure to burn as well.

Once he was in the cave he went immediately to the shrine and dug through the wall. Taking his precious cargo with him, he entered the great cavern and again sealed the hole. He knew his window of opportunity was short, so he immediately set to work. He had wrapped his food in some leaves when he first came into the cavern, and he now took up one of the broader ones. He carefully emptied the pitcher out onto the floor until one of the big bugs tumbled free. It immediately scuttled away. Petron was on it in a flash. It stopped when he approached and threatened him, appendages up. Petron was in no mood to trifle. He scooped it up and wrapped it in the leaf. He secured it tightly, knowing where it would soon be going. He went back to the pitcher and repeated dumping. A second bug tumbled free, and Petron caught and wrapped this one also. The rest of the sand came out of the pitcher with no bugs, but one other thing did fall out: a thumb-sized round crystal. Petron recalled seeing it when he first encountered the burial ground. He examined it and saw it was a ring cut from clear stone. He tried it on, and found it fit his smallest finger. It was no surprise to him that it was cut in the shape of a shark.

Petron stood and faced the wall art. His heart was pounding. The magic had told him how to interpret the drawings, and it confirmed what he had suspected. When the black bugs were taken into the body under the influence of magic, they could transform the human body. If they were swallowed whole, the transformation was complete, and permanent; the man would become an animal. If a woman were to insert one inside herself as she would take in a man, she would join the ranks of the mer-people forever. If, however, the bug was inserted up one's backside, the spell was temporary, and the person would revert to being human, provided that nothing from the sea was consumed while the person was transformed. This was Petron's goal. He was just loathe to follow the method. He knew, however, that he had no choice. The magic had also shown him one other thing; the well in the cave had no bottom. More precisely, it was a channel that led to the sea. If he could transform into a fish, he could leave that way and the villagers would never see him again.

Petron studied the two insects he had wrapped. He guessed that the task would be easiest with the smaller one. He carefully took the larger and set it aside in one of the niches. As a precaution, he covered it with sand, to keep it moist in case he needed it. Petron then carefully put the smaller one in a niche beside it. He went and filled the pitcher with water, and washed himself off, then filled it again and drank. He took the fish that he had left and rubbed it over his hands until they were as greasy as possible. Clearing a space in front of the drawings, Petron studied them one last time, in case any other ideas came to his mind. Finally, after double checking the placement of the two bugs, Petron took the largest crystal and lifted it over his head. He hesitated a moment, then lowered it. Realizing that sharp bits of flying crystal might cut him, Petron moved the other crystal around in front of him, to hide his feet. He then closed his eyes, heaved the stone prism high, and smashed it to the ground.

The first time Petron smashed a crystal, it had been an accident. This time the effort was far more deliberate, and the result more gratifying. As before, the stone shard exploded into a cloud of dust and fragments. Petron could feel the electric buzz on his skin instantly. He bent down and quickly inhaled, and just as quickly exploded into a coughing fit. The coughing subsided much more quickly this time, however, to be replaced with a greatly heightened awareness. What had seemed like wisps before were full specters now, the aspect of wizards and kings long past. Others were there, more fantastic still, with alien countanance and tongue. Together they all spoke to him of magic, and destiny. He saw the threat facing him. On one hand lay the magic with its power to maim and enslave. On the other hand were the villagers who were already beginning to realize that their quarry was no longer trapped in the remains of the scrub. Petron stared both sides down and chose to continue.

With a wave of his hand Petron summoned a blast of air that swept the shards of crystal aside and set the cloud of stone to dancing, lifting the stones just a bit off the cave floor. He stared at the drawings, and at the bugs in their niches. He was not entirely surprised to see a tiny spark of light inside each of the bugs. He could hear the chants of the wizards so long ago as they first crafted this enchantment to change men into beasts and women to fishes. To his surprise and delight the crystal on his finger was also aglow now. In a heartbeat, he knew what it was for; a wizard long ago had made it as a ward against the mer-people, and against sea life in general. It was marvelously made, he could see that now; its beauty brought tears to his eyes. He then remembered where he found the ring, and he clenched his fist around it in memory of the shallow graves in the ruins.

Petron took up the black bug, wrapped in its leaf. He could sense that it was still alive. Petron took a deep breath. Infused as he was with the magic, he could see now what he was facing. Once inside his body, the bug would sting, and sting, and sting again. The venom could dissolve flesh, and that's exactly what would happen to him. The magic would reshape his body as the venom loosened it. He needed to know what his goal was, envisioning it in his mind, and allow the magic and the venom to work the transformation. In his mind's eye, he could already see Temma's father turning away from the dying fire that had swept the last of the scrub away, and in his inner hearing he could hear the crunch of his footsteps as he started towards the cave. Time was short --

best to get started.

Petron took the tiny package in his fingers and rubbed some of the grease off his hands and onto the wrapping. He then squatted and with hesitant touch placed the package down deep between his legs. Once it was in place he started to press it in. He tried to handle it by the wrap, to avoid crushing the insect, but that was difficult. He could feel it, in his mind, with the magic he had inhaled, and so he used that magic now to push it in deeper. The pressure mounted as he pushed it harder and deeper. It felt like the worse bowel movement he had ever had, only in reverse. A wave of nausea struck him as he forced it past the sphincter and in. He toppled over backward with his legs spayed apart. It was in. Petron slowly and carefully climbed to his feet. He could feel the insect inside him struggling to free itself of the wrapping; whether by actual sensation or magically he was not sure. Petron pictured the black bug in his mind, and pictured it gently slipping free of the leaf. He was sure he could feel it moving inside him. Petron decided that he wanted to be as close as possible to the well when the change happened. Taking care to not change the angle of his stance, Petron stiffly lurched forward, moving toward the elevated cloud of stone, and then suddenly doubled up in agony as his entire viscera ignited in a massive spasm of pain.

One time in his life Petron had made the mistake of accidentally upending a pot of boiling water on himself. He had been in his early teens and reckless, and had knocked the pot off a tripod while trying to slip past someone. He had been wearing short breaches at the time, and the boiling water splashed over his shins and feet. He had never felt so much pain before or since, until now. It felt as if someone had dumped that pot of boiling water inside his guts, and this time there was no one nearby with a pail of water to cool him. He fell to the floor howling incoherently. The muscles of his torso and legs convulsed uncontrollable. He lost control of his bowels in one explosive movement, voiding the bug and its wrapper. He tried to crawl towards the well, which now seemed leagues away, while bawling and weeping. Part of his mind told him that he needed to take control of the situation if he wanted to live, but that was a very small part. Most of his mind was blank with pain.

After what felt like an eon, but which was really just a few heartbeats, the pain started to fade, replaced by a leaden feeling of weight. That tiny part of Petron's brain told him his guts were falling numb, and likely starting to dissolve. Fear seized his mind, and panic, but he drove them both away and focused desperately on the image of Temma's mother. The pain made it very hard to concentrate, but he forced himself again and again to picture her in her blue-skinned glory, with talons and webbing and scales and those deadly sharp teeth. The magic was still with him, and light swirled in his vision. Ghostly faces gaped at him, and he seized those with his mind and turned them into mer-people also, until a sea of naked, scaled bipeds swam about him. Now he could feel the toxin washing through his veins, and to his horror his diaphragm seized, leaving him without even the strength to gasp for air. He reached out with the magic and pushed the air into his lungs, again and again. Knowing what would come next, he willed his heart to keep beating even as a pain just as sharp and hard as a knife stabbed in his chest. He held the image of Temma's mother in his mind, and willed himself to live, and to change.

Amid his agony, he heard voices again, muffled by stone. The villagers had reached the shrine. He lifted himself on numb arms and struggled towards the well. Behind him he heard the sound of arguing. He collapsed again, exhausted, and just willed breath and blood to flow while he imagined himself as a merman. In response unseen hands tugged and pushed at his innards. What followed was just a blank moment of sheer agony. Then the pain subsided, and after several heartbeats he could feel his chest moving on its own again. The sound of stone being moved kicked him back into action. He lifted himself up on his arms and resumed crawling, slipping under the dancing rocks. Petron was pleased to realize his legs still worked, and he kicked against the cave floor. This sped things up a bit, but also allowed him to realize that the skin all over his body was burning. He wondered if he was on fire, blazing like a signal torch. Overhead the cloud of stone slowly danced in the air, providing some cover. Behind him he heard stones falling, and Temma's father shouting. Petron imagined himself all blue and covered in scales, swimming freely in the warm ocean. Again his insides writhed, and he blacked out. The sound of rockfall jolted him awake again, and Petron pulled and kicked with all his might, his talons gripping the rock beneath him. More rock fell, more distant now, and then there came the sound of bodies scrabbling over stones.

From behind him Petron heard orders being shouted, and the sound of feet slapping the floor. Petron pictured himself as a full mer-man, blue scales wet over smooth muscles and iron sinews. A spasm of pain jolted Petron off his feet, dropping him back on his belly. Shouts followed, and he could hear the village men running up on either side of the cloud of rock. Through the pain Petron felt a different sensation; he felt different: tighter, better. The transformation was nearing completion. The ghosts swirled around his head and nodded affirmation. Once last wave of pain and nausea hit him as his privates seemed to turn inside out and crawl inside his belly. He wanted to grab them and pull them back out, but he could not spare the motion. Instead Petron danced up onto webbed hands and feet and dashed forward like a four-legged crab. Shouts came again, falling behind now. The cloud of stone fell behind as Petron caught sight of the well. A single villager stood guard, club raised: Temma's father. Petron tossed himself erect with a single hand, blue-skinned legs pumping like pistons, and looked the man right in the eye. Thin blue lips parted over a serrated smile when Petron saw the fear in the man's eyes. Petron could feel inside himself enough speed and strength to take the man's life and still complete the mission, and for an instant he pondered the justice of that. Then Temma's face came unbidden to his mind, and Petron leaped lightly over the man's head, easily avoiding the blow aimed at where he had been. The water's surface fell at him just long enough to breathe a prayer of thanks, and then Petron sliced cleanly into the world.

It was as if Petron had never opened his eyes until then, or had never heard anything until then. It was like pulling a blindfold off that had been there his entire life, and he was now seeing for the first time. The water carried sound and smell and taste and light like no summer day had ever done so before. It was heaven. In an instant Petron knew where to go. The well narrowed sharply for a few chains, then widened and flattened. It was dark but Petron had no problem seeing. He swam like a thought crosses a mind. There was no current to fight, no seaweed to slow his progress. The water grew cold, then grew warmer again. A glimmer of light appeared, far in the distance, and that drew Petron on even harder. It was like a race, but with no other runners. The mouth of the cave opened up, and Petron shot out into the clear blue ocean.

Only when Petron reached the open water did he slow, and stop to think. He was suddenly shocked to realize that he had not even paused to consider how he could navigate the pitch-black tunnel. He looked down at his body and took in the changes. He was indeed a mer-man now. The change was more than appearance. He could hear so much better now, and taste. He was actually breathing the water! He noticed a glow coming from one hand, and saw the ring. The magic was still infusing him, and he knew that the ring was actively warding off any large sea predators. The sense of the magic was fading, partly because time had passed since he smashed the crystal, and partly because the change to mer-man had clouded his mind to human things even as it sharpened his animal senses. The dark whispers still drifted through his mind, but now they were just noise. Petron suddenly felt hungry, and now the magic started to feel more intense. There was a danger here, Petron remembered; the magic was offering him a choice. To eat of the sea was to choose the sea. Even though his method of invoking the change was intended to allow the change to be temporary, eating anything of the sea, while under this guise, would render the change permanent. Petron considered this, and decided he needed to make one last trip to the village.

Petron drove hard toward the surface. Breaching, he looked about and spotted the village. He set off for it, his new form slicing through the water. Faster than he could have run the distance, Petron swam it. When the water got too shallow to swim, he climbed out and walked, spitting out the water in his lungs. With the magic in his mind, the village looked a bit different. He could now see the totems and charms for what they were, and the spirit face outside the healer's hut shown like a beacon. Petron ignored them and went instead to the fire-pit where the tubers were roasted. Sure enough, there were several roasted roots there. Petron took one and bit into it. He found it quite easy to eat, although no more appetizing than before. The salted fish beckoned, but he ignored it. He took two more tubers and turned to go back to the water. He found the way blocked by two of the older girls, their eyes huge in shock and horror. Petron looked down at himself. He was as naked as they were, but he was no longer as human. His skin was slick with iridescent blue scales, and his webbed hands now sported black talons instead of nails. He knew by feel that his teeth were now as sharp as shark teeth, and his tongue was much longer. Even his male parts had changed, retracted inside his now-hairless belly, hidden from any nibbling sea creature. He expected that his pupils were now slitted, just as Temma's mother's had been. Oddly, none of this bothered him. He stepped towards the two girls, who shrank back slowly, clutching each other. He leaned forward, and in his best islander said: "Go." They both shrieked in terror, and fled. Petron walked unhindered back to the sea. He cast a last glance back over his shoulder at the village and saw several the older girls standing and pointing. He thought perhaps the old healer was among them, but he didn't bother making sure. The water was calling now, calling seductively and strongly. Petron waded in up to his shins, then dove.

As Petron swam he realized that the magic was fading from his mind. Before that could happen, he sought a way to reverse the change. It seemed that time alone was sufficient to affect the conversion back to a man, but Petron did not trust in that. The essence of his humanity was in himself, but its return could be hastened. Petron focused on that essence, collecting it. He saw the tubers still in his hand. He drew that essence, concentrated it, and placed it in one of the tubers. This weakened the magic remaining, but there was still enough left to sense the direction to the mainland. It was quite a way off, but Petron felt strong, and the water was warm even by human standards. As he swam Petron thought about the pirates, and about Temma. With the canoes burned, and with the island burned, they would be forced to abandon their pirate ways. They could probably escape well enough to the mainland, or to one of the larger islands. The threat they posed was gone, and Temma could have a chance to grow up in normal society, or as normal a society as any of these lands had.

The sights, sounds, smells, and sensations of the ocean filled and aroused Petron as he swam. He threaded though the coral outcroppings with their multi-hued fish and sea-life, always headed for the mainland but always looking, always watching, always listening. He tasted the stones on the bottom, felt the sun filtering down, heard the grinding of the fine grit of the sand as his swift passage stirred it up. The lure of the sea was strong, but his time on the island had stiffened his resolve, and Petron kept his focus on the mainland. He swam until he was tired, then found an outcropping to stand up on. To his surprise, when he surfaced, there was no land to be seen. He ate the un-enchanted tuber for strength, and dove in again. Not long afterward he came to the end of the coral, and the sea floor fell away to dark abysses. It was on the edge of that abyss that Petron spotted the wreck. He turned and dove down to it, feeling the depth compressing his bones. It was the front half of a ship, wedged between the slope and a large boulder. Petron checked the bow for a name. He found one, but to his bemusement he could no longer read it. He flitted in and out of the rent hull, searching for clues of identity. He cast about, examining the nearby debris. All of it was familiar, but none of it was conclusive. He hung before it, suspended on a stray current of water, listening to the sounds of mysterious life on the darkness far below. He had left his life on the island, and he had also left his life on that ship. All that remained was the life of the sea, as a fish or as a man. He had chosen to be a man, and that was right. Satisfied, Petron swam on towards shore.

CHAPTER SEVEN

The Pier

The morning sun had barely appeared above the trees across the lagoon but the air was already thick with heat. The water of the lagoon lazily lapped at the sand and there was no wind. Seagulls soared overhead, small black marks against the blue, but none of their calls reached the village. Small sounds of everyday life came from the nearest houses. The fishing boats had all left for the day, taking most of the village men with them, and whichever women had the energy to work were working under shade of tree or hut. The village was alive, but not bustling.

Linot stood at the end of the pier, his hands working at mending a torn fishing net. This was not his usual labor, but his father and the chief were sequestered with the other elders deep in the forest, planning the rituals for the summer festival, and Linot had already completed most of the easier chores for the day. He needed a place to stretch out the net, to show him where all the tears were, and the pier was unused once the boats left.

As his hands worked to weave the new fiber into the net, Linot's mind was free to wander. He reviewed in his mind the scene from several days before of the foreign ship being rowed out of the harbor by the strange men from the north. Linot had been working on fixing a broken paddle and had a good opportunity to watch the scene. He had marveled at the variety of colors of hair and shapes of bodies in the crew of the foreign ship as they lowered their strange boat with the narrow paddles and towed the larger ship out of the harbor. Earlier he had overheard a conversation about how the crew had picked up a few new sailors in local ports, and he wondered which of the light-skinned men manning the oars were new.

Linot had occasionally wondered what it would be like to sail away, to leave the island behind and explore the world. As the son of the scribe he knew all the stories and heard all the news that came to the island, and he knew there was more to life than fishing and nets and carving fetishes. He also knew, all too well now, the dangers that the world held. There was something to be said for staying in familiar waters.

The sun was almost at zenith when Linot finished the net. He carefully gathered it up and started rolling it so it could be stowed. He had almost finished when he heard fast footfalls and looked up to see two of the village monks running toward him. In their hands were spears, their metal points glistening in the sunlight. Linot stood, paralyzed, too shocked to even call out and ask what he had done to attract such unwanted attention. The two other men were almost upon him before he realized they were not running at him, but were instead running toward the pier. Linot turned to watch them run past and leap up on the pier, and as he did so he caught sight for the first time of the boat coming into the harbor. He dropped the net and ran up the pier after the monks.

Almost immediately Linot knew the boat was not one of their own. It was not a dugout, but a reed boat, made of many floating stems bound together. As the boat drew closer, propelled both by the wind and by the paddling of the crew, Linot also realized this was not a warship, but just a fishing vessel. A warship would not be carrying the fishing gear and baskets. This seemed to be an unusual fishing expedition, however, for Linot could see that the crew of this ship seemed to include women and children. The monks could also see that this ship was not a threat worthy of spears, and as the boat drew near the pier they lay the weapons aside and helped the overburdened ship dock.

The first strangers off the ship were fishermen and sailors, who brought the ship in closer to the pier and lashed it in place. They then helped the women and children off the boat. One of the monks, Bolan by name, approached one of the sailors as they worked.

"Where are you from?" Bolan asked.

"We are from Klaggit," the man said. Linot recognized that as an island on the far side of Sanduha, a neighboring island. "But these," he indicated the women and children, "are from the mainland."

Linot looked the strangers over critically. Several times a year, traders from the mainland would visit his father, and these people looked nothing like those traders. Their hair was styled differently, cut short in a crude fashion, and their tattoos were different. Most of them were naked, just like himself and the fishermen. He could see now that a couple of the men he had assumed were sailors were actually mainlanders, because they were now standing with the women and children in a huddle in the middle of the pier, looking down at the gathering villagers with some apprehension. Linot hearkened back to his adventure fishing with Mundan, and his stomach tightened at the thought that he had not needed to venture from his own home to come face to face with the mysteries of the world.

"How did you come to find mainlanders, and why did you bring them here?" asked Bolan.

"We found them at sea, in a small vessel. It was breaking up, and sinking, and they could no longer steer it." The sailor threw a quick glance at one of his crewmates. "Some of us wanted to help them. Some of us wanted ..." He looked down. "We agreed to rescue them." He looked up again, his expression tired. "By the time we got them all on board we found that we could no longer sail against the currents back to our own island. Your island was the first we could reach."

Linot looked over the strangers. They looked thin, as if they had not been eating well of late. He approached them, and the tallest of the mainlander men turned to face him.

"How long were you at sea?" Linot asked. The tall man looked at Linot, his expression puzzled. After a long pause he spoke.

"We were at sea long time," he said, his accent very pronounced and his grammar abbreviated. At his side stood an old woman dressed in a grass shawl. The old woman beckoned to a naked little girl who stood nearby.

"Temma," the old woman called, and the girl came to her and clutched her tightly. The woman's accent drew the girl's name out, making it sound more like "Temmmlaa". The girl stared at Linot with a steady but wary gaze.

Another monk approached them. "It is clear that you found these people for a reason," he said to the sailors. The monk was named Hared, and he was the servant of the priest. "You were meant to bring them here. How else would you have found them in the vastness of the ocean?"

"This must be true," Bolan said, nodding. He turned to the strangers. "Are you hungry?"

The tall man looked reluctantly at his people, who looked back expectantly at him. Linot could see hesitation in his posture, as if his pride would not allow him to ask for help, but the young girl did not hesitate. She nodded vigorously.

"Yes," echoed the old woman, also in a thick accent. The tall man threw her a sour look, but then his expression softened and he nodded as well.

"Come," Hared said, gesturing toward the village and walking past the clustered mainlanders. "We will feed you." He turned back to the fishermen. "Thank you for bringing our new friends here. We will feed you, too." The fishermen looked at each other, shrugged, and nodded as well. Everyone started walking toward the village, although the mainlanders seemed to lag, some almost stumbling as they walked.

Linot walked ahead of the group with the monks. At the end of the pier he jumped down, then stopped. He looked back at the pier, where the little girl stood. She stopped at the end of the pier, looking uncertainly at the step down and at the village beyond.

"Do you need help?" Linot asked.

The girl frowned, crossing her thin arms over her bare, brown chest and wobbling slightly as she stood. Finally she nodded, and reached out both hands. Linot reached out his hands, and she fell into his arms. Her body was too light, and bony, and in the heat of the day her skin seemed too dry, but she felt otherwise normal, much like any other girl would. Linot eased her to the ground, and she quickly shuffled a few steps away, then turned and looked back at the pier. There stood the old woman. Linot could see that her wrinkled skin was decorated with myriad fish scales, drawn all over her legs and belly. Linot reached up his hands, offering to help her down. She accepted his offer, and took his hands. When she did, Linot felt a shock, almost like an insect sting, and his knees quivered. He almost dropped her hands, but she kept her grip, and did not seem to notice. She hopped off the pier, and Linot had to choose between easing her fall and having her land on him. He chose the former. Once she was down he dropped her hands and backed up a step, his eyes wide. He stared at her as she motioned to the girl.

"Temnla, come," she said, and the girl took her hand. The duo turned toward the village. Linot just stood, too shocked to move, the nerves in his hands twanging and his fingers twitching. For a horrible moment he was back at sea, on a desert island with a creature he had never seen before. He could do nothing but stare as the foreigners calmly and quietly invaded his village.

ACKNOWLEDGEMENT

Many people helped me write this book, and I want to call out a few folks who really were key. I want to thank my sweet Naomi for her love, support, and encouragement. Thanks go to Fiona and Joanie for their comments and proofreading, and of course I could not have written and finished this work without the help and guidance of Liam, Jon, Daf, Joe, and the other folks from the Dargon Project.

ABOUT THE AUTHOR

James Owens

Jim Owens is the third of seven children, so if you meet him offer him food. He started writing as a boy, creating hand-illustrated stories on construction paper. He then progressed to an ancient typewriter that cut holes in the paper whenever he typed an "O" or a "0". He currently uses a computer for his word processing, which he keeps in his home in Ohio, which he shares with his loving wife and a transient population of friends, family, cats, and roving insects. He is also a founding member of the Dargon Project, the oldest collaborative writing project on the Internet.